A SPIRIT'S LAST GIFT

A WINTER NOVELLA

KATHY-LYNN CROSS

INSCYTHEFUL PUBLISHING

INSCYTHEFUL PUBLISHING

Ebook ISBN# 978-1-7337890-1-1
Print ISBN# 978-1-7337890-0-4
Story, original formatting and cover by
Kathy-Lynn Cross
Editing by Amber Hassler
Published by Inscytheful Publishing

YA: A wintry novella dealing with loss, paranormal problems, and the fear of love.

❄

Dedicated to the ones who complete their other half.
Thank you for being mine, Jeffrey.
Merry Christmas.

PROLOGUE

December 23rd, 2016.

G*asp.*
> One breath.
> *Choke.*

Another.

Cough.

Then two more involuntary shallow intakes helped me to realign this reality. There was a hint of chill mixed with the aroma of damp earth and flesh vegetation decay. I rocked my head back and forth within the tiny confinement to gain clarity. Ever since the misunderstanding, it's been this way every night.

Reluctant, I wiggled each toe, before extending both arms out of the crisscross placement over my chest while relaxing each finger. As I shifted, my brain invented the whisper of silk moving against polyester and Lycia. The fabrication, of fictional dress material, gave me some reassurance; this was very real. Following this new routine, I forced my lashes to flutter open. Going through the physical motions made me feel displaced; especially after I woke to ivory silk seven inches above my face.

When the moon rose at 9:02 p.m., so did I.

Who knew, that time had a sense of humor?

Let's Chat for a bit.

Before I share my story, there are a few things I would like to make clear. And, before you go there, I do not use bendy straws to suck blood. I don't crave Brains on a Half Skull. Nor am I a full-blooded angel or misplaced demon. Although my Keeper, Haste, told me certain nightmares do exist because, he—in fact—is one of them.

Haste had introduced himself right after my first awakening when he yanked me from my coffin. But what I'll never forget was when the weight of this new transition sunk in as I watched the snowflakes pass through my hands and fingertips. My Keeper then proceeded to explain when a soul passes with unresolved regret, anger, or desires, the human psyche fractures. This information was unfortunate because, at the time of departure, my baggage was crammed to capacity and had left a massive amount of emotional residue behind. And if the soul becomes chain-laden, the bond can keep the soul tethered in between the physical plain and what lies beyond.

If you haven't pieced it together by now, I am a Layer, or in layman's terms, a spirit stuck in limbo. I desired someone close to me but kept him at arm's length most of my life. And if I were honest, being in love with him truly scared me, to the point that I hated myself. *Anger, check. Desire, check. Regret, double check.*

So, in the end, you *can* take certain things with you. With my last breath, I looped one arm through my anger and the other around my one regrettable secret. Together they escorted me to the grave.

My name is Juslynn Ann Vaxton and this is how my existence moved from Bothell, Washington to Bothell Cemetery, plot number 1218.

CHAPTER ONE

Saturday, December 17th, 2016.

The sluggish warmth that tingled from fingertips to knuckles relaxed me as my cousin shuffled about her workstation prepping it for my hand massage. Her shocking pink hair tapered in a zig-zag, stair-like pattern, starting from her temples and rounded to the back of her head. This latest expression of her individuality had me gawking. Surprisingly, enough of the color helped her complexion and softened her chiseled nose and chin.

She turned up her iPod and hummed along with the latest tune from T. Swift. I realized my stiff posture had crumbled toward the table as my shoulders rolled forward. The weary pleasure from shopping caught me by surprise, and I stifled a yawn. There was much to do before tomorrow night. Scooting to the back of the chair, I forced myself to sit straight and shake off the fatigue.

Two small bottles of Silver and Sapphire glittered under her work lamp. The sparkle diminished my sleepy smile a tad.

I should be ecstatic. It was my senior year. I was pulling decent enough grades and had received three letters of acceptance, one of which was to our state's university. I had superb parents; well technically, Karia was my step-mother, but she did her best, and I gave her full marks for trying. It was hard stepping into the shoes of a departed wife and mother, and my mom's shoes were pretty spectacular.

After winter break, we were going to car shop with some of the inheritance my mom left me when I turn eighteen in January. The car would serve as a daily reminder she was still caring for me. I had also asked my dad if I could pull extra money out to detail angel wings on the back window since my mom was obsessed with them, and a personalized license plate because I had picked out the car's name too, *Cerena*. He thought my mom would get a kick out of it, and Karia told me it was a wonderful idea.

The car was a necessity and not a selfish want. I was starting my first job in January. *See, I should be bursting with glee, except for missing my mom.* Life was coming together for me. And yet, the one thing on my list that was giving me roller-coaster anxiety... I was going to the Snow Flurry Dance, with Carter.

Carter's family, which included his strict father and his father's brother, moved here when he was in third grade. When the teacher introduced him to the class is when my secret took root. Even though we had started off as fast friends, the innocent crush I carried for him blossomed into desire our second year of high school. To my shock, I've managed to keep it safely guarded from everyone, including him. The fear of jeopardizing our friendship helps to keep my emotions in check. My motto: Pour the milk into a bucket and freeze it. Then it can never spill if it gets knocked over, and I won't have to mend a shattered heart either.

Our friendship was an ongoing adventure. We made it through the chicken pox disaster at age nine by playing Connect-the-Dots with a permanent marker. I can't recall who had come up with the idea first, but both of us found ourselves grounded for a month. But buddies like us still found a way to communicate, by way of messenger cat. We tied notes to his cat Chirp's tail.

When Carter turned thirteen, he showed up to class with braces. I laughed so hard I ended up in the counselor's office and reprimanded for disrupting the class. Then to add insult to injury, Karma bit me in the butt because two weeks later I caught metal mouth. Carter used to tease me and say things like, "Don't stand too close, we might shock one another now." Shortly after, we started a support group and called ourselves, Metal Talk, where we consoled friends who ended up wired with the ability to pick up Wi-Fi. Even though we left four years ago, I heard our junior high had kept the group going.

I thought of myself as mousy and believed my best friend's sinful, good looks evened out my blandness. For example, Carter's choppy raven locks, to my long, straight chestnut hair. He was 6'1", and I stopped growing at 5'5 ½". But, I made up my shortcoming by wearing heels.

We were totally opposite in eye color; mine being a deep brown-black, but in the winter, seemed black more than brown, whereas Carter's were sunlit blue all year round. If the sunlight caught the color, just so, I could make out silver flakes. It reminded me of snow falling, which added one more thing I loved about him since winter was my favorite time of year.

I focused on the floating glitter in the silver nail polish

bottle. Blue, silver-flecked eyes materialized, between my long-drawn-out blinks. Then his slightly crooked nose formed. In my mind, I followed his features down past the Cupid's bow, and stopped at his mouth, as it pulled into a melt-your-virtue-away half smirk, exposing one of his dimples.

His face was inches from mine when the present boomeranged once my cousin's Boston laced words bounced off of my eardrums. "J-baby? Hey hon, where did you go?" Sassy snapped her neon gum. "Ya know a mind is a dangerous place if you wander around for too long." She tapped both wrists with her favorite four-way file. "I need you here because I don't know what your dress looks like and if I should match the pattern of your nails to the dress." She chewed, while assessing my actions, then popped her gum again.

My chest ached as I released the trapped air in an exhausted sigh. I had no idea how guarding specific emotions could physically drain a person. The plastic smile I glued on was as fake as my nails. It gave the illusion I was fine, and I used the generic excuse to my advantage.

With a one-shoulder shrug, I nonchalantly answered, "Sassy, I'm all right. I was rethinking my shoes. I bought them on a whim before purchasing the dress." The real reason I wanted to swap out the heels was because my original prom date, Peter, was shorter than Carter. The two-inch heels made me the right height for us to dance comfortably. But before my cousin could interject on my backward way of shopping, I added, "I think the color and the height of the heel won't do the dress justice and accentuate the slit."

I paused, recalculating the difference between Peter's 5'11" and Carter's 6'1". Adding two more inches to my height would place me right below Carter's chin. I frowned. Returning them for a different pair was essential.

Thinking about why I needed to switch the shoes made my heart do flip-flops. I couldn't believe Carter and I were actually going, as friends sure, but we would be together… like a couple. Heat flashed across both cheeks, and in seconds I knew my heart was about to betray our secret. Quickly, I dropped my gaze as strands of hair shielded the sides of my face.

I was pathetic, assuming one of my wishing stars must have intervened and messed with our fate because Peter came down with the flu and had been absent for two days. We weren't a couple, but he had formally asked me to be his date, and it would've been my first one. *Ever.* My answer made me feel disloyal in about six different ways, but I couldn't keep waiting for a certain someone to ask me. Besides, I figured saying yes to Peter would get back to Carter because they were both on the varsity hockey team. The plan was to flick the jealousy switch, but it backfired. Instead, it cranked out a new rumor. Infecting everyone's mouth was how he asked Cynthia Masterson after he heard from Peter I had agreed to go with him. But as the chain of events went down, I figured he had planned to ask her all along and chalked it up to mere coincidence.

However, as Mom would say, "Never say never."

Before the pep-rally the cheer squad decided to practice, Cynthia was one of the supports on the pyramid. The top girl freaked out. Something about her contact popping out, and lost her balance. The pile of cheerleaders tumbled to the ground. One of the girls broke Cyn's right femur when she landed on top of it, with both feet.

Picturing the scene in my head made me shudder when I mentally heard the snap. I would never have wished for something that horrible to happen so I could have a chance with

Carter. However, as I said, it was Fate's plan unfolding on mine.

I called up my best friend to inform him about Peter's bad luck bug and that I was going to order pizza and hang out with Spaz. Then he told me about Cynthia's rotten dilemma. Internally, my Cheshire cat was grinning, but at the same time expressed how sorry their situations were. In a rush, he suggested we should go together. I covered the phone's mic, and scanned the bedroom for my fairy godmother, but only saw my corgi, Spaz, sleeping in his bed.

Once I answered him, my tongue stuck to the roof of my mouth, making normal conversation impossible. So, he wouldn't realize my dilemma; I gave him one-word answers. The last thing I remembered was him asking if I was all right and like a star-struck fan I whimpered, "Uh-huh." He ended the call with a velvety snicker.

We were going to the dance together.

"Earth to Cuz."

Wonderful, I spaced out again. Blinking Sassy into focus, I stated frankly, "I should have picked something with a higher heel."

"Uh-Huh." Her eyebrow arched. She wasn't buying it, but proceeded to dry off my hands, then started to rub scented oil on both thumb cuticles. "I heard, this December is supposed to be colder than normal. And you know, Morning's with Mike, the morning radio show?"

I bobbed my head.

"Mike said there was a forty percent chance of snow tonight and throughout tomorrow. Merry Early Christmas. I can't wait to go ice skating." She chewed fast then popped her gum several times.

"And?"

"Oh, yeah, right. Anyway, you might want to rethink the heels, J-baby."

Her advice reeked, causing me to wrinkle my nose at her involuntarily. "Geez, I've been wearing heels since I was eleven. I know how to handle myself in them. Besides, I'm not running the hundred-yard dash, although I do plan on dancing."

"Maybe pick out a new pair of galoshes to go with your outfit, and change at the dance?"

Picturing the laced hem of the dress wet from slush, and who could guess how far across the parking lot we would have to walk, then up the stairs to the gym where the dance was being held. The vision ruined my idea of the perfect date appearance. And I knew I didn't have a magical mother with a Bibbidi-Boo dress for me to change into at the dance. I was going to take this opportunity to cast my own spell on Carter. Then he would notice me for more than a childhood friend, library buddy, or understanding fill-in when one of his dates canceled.

A lanky redhead waddled up to the table in paper flip-flops, saving me from releasing the rebuttal burning on the tip of my tongue. Even though Sassy was my friend by relation default and manicurist, she more than likely would have taken offense to the smartass comment I had locked behind my teeth. She's been known for retaliating with a possible nail smudge or innocently forgetting the quick dry topcoat, to leave you tacky.

"Juslynn, what do you think of this color on my toes?" Fern shook her firelocks in genuine concern while creating a serious faux pas. I loved her fashion innocence. She was a blank canvas. Electric green eyes, pale skin, but not so pale you would label her Sparkly. Freckles dusted across the bridge of her nose and shoulders. And like a leopard, she was never ashamed to show off her spots. The strapless hunter green dress she purchased proved it.

Fern Swanson wiggled her French tipped toes. Her frown deepened waiting for my approval.

"You got a French manicure. It's basic, and will show off your gold pumps perfectly."

Her scowl deepened. "But what about the details I had done?"

Squinting, I leaned over without disturbing Sassy's massage. "What did you have done?"

"Mistletoe. On both of my big toes. I added something Christmassy. Don't you see the green leaves and three berries? Misty made them smaller than normal. Do you think it will take away from the dress?"

Hiding the smirk that threatened to expose what I really thought, I cleared my throat instead. "Um, those are holly berries. But don't worry, I think your toes scream, 'Deck the Halls; I'm here to party and wish Lander's would get a clue and kiss me.'"

The pink frown was back but started sinking into her face creating a seamless pout. "You think so? I had a feeling it was too much."

Sassy couldn't take it anymore. "Your toes are happy to be dressed up and going to the dance. I think you are going to rock it tomorrow night. Who finally asked you?"

Fern's freckles deepened from a natural blush. "Wade Lander."

A low whistle came from my cousin. "He's quite the catch. Football player, right?"

Fern's eyes lit up. "Yes, tight end. Number forty-seven."

Someone smacked me between my shoulder blades with what felt like a rolled-up magazine. From the hollow air thunk, I would say it was a Cosmo, which meant Britney Grister was behind me.

Without turning my head to acknowledge her, I said, "Hi, Brie." The greeting came out terse as I tried not to knock over the bowls my hands were soaking in.

Traces of peroxide and ammonia tickled my nose before a cascade of medium wavy copper-toned hair with new blond highlights fell down the side of my face. Her snickers intensified in my ear as she planted a lip-gloss peck on my temple. One would assume she was pleased with the way her hair had come out. Brie wasn't cursing about it, and that was a huge plus.

Britney bumped the side of the table causing some of the tepid oily water to slosh over. Sassy groaned dabbing the unprotected areas near the light's base and nail polish display tower. Fern snickered, as I apologized for Brie's electric hips.

"Sorry, she short-circuits when she gets excited."

"Just!"

I cringed at her generic nickname. "What? I'm only disclosing what's on your warning tag."

Sassy pulled out a couple of dry towels. Rearranging her workstation, she pulled the magnifying lamp over to position it above my hand. Then gave the girls' the two-handed 'shoo-shoo' gesture. Both stepped back, and when Sassy approved of their distance, she turned her attention back to me.

"Okay. So, tell me about your dress."

Fern jumped forward. "You should see the sequin detailing and the fabric is ninety percent Polyester and ten percent Lycra. The color is royal blue with the same color lace overlay that helps emphasize the scoop neckline." Then she bent over to draw the slit as she described it. "Oh, and the sexy slit stops right at the top of the left thigh. And the cashmere opera floor-length cape, with a white faux fox, trimmed around the hood…"

Three sets of eyes bore into Fern's face.

Unable to help myself, I worked at feigning irritation, but between each word a slight giggle slipped out. "So, tell me, Fern, how do you really feel about my choice?"

With one hand on her hip, tapping a paper flip-flop, and pointing her index finger in my face. "Look you. I would have bought it if I had the chunk to fill in the bodice."

"Chunk?" The three of us stared.

"Yeah. You know?" Fern held her hands out four inches from her B cup chest and smiled. "See, chunk."

"Well, how should I take that Mickey Mouse complement? I'm fat enough to fill the dress, or you admire my C shelf?"

Fern turned as red as her hair causing us to laugh. Then the bell on the shop's door clinked against the glass. We watched Cher Louis approach the front desk. The room filled with her presence, encircling us with the scent of old money, which smelled spoiled.

The Louis family owned various stores down Main Street, one bed and breakfast, and donated lumber to build the new High School's gym. They figured since their family lineage dated back five generations, the town owed them for keeping everyone afloat. The town knew it was hogwash but publicly stating the obvious would put your name in their black book. *How did I know this?* My family was in it.

My dad owned the Vaxton newspaper, only because his father left it to him. There was a misunderstanding between Cher's grandfather and mine. For some reason, they thought when my grandfather passed the business was being left to him and his family to run. Leaving it to his son, Dave, was a smart move on my grandfather's part;

Bothell would have gone from Wall Street style news to the Enquirer.

Also, their family was a little on the cracked side. Most of them believed they had the ability of foresight. Cher tried to steer clear from that side of her family. Unfortunately, her mother was a believer. When Cher received her license, she distanced herself from both, her mother and grandmother. Even though I felt bad for her, there was no friendship lost between us. She still made my life miserable.

Her spray tan had faded. In specific areas on her face, it appeared brassy under the natural lighting in the shop. Cher's long oversized gray sweater stimulated one's imagination until you noticed her black skinny jeans; she was a size two. I envied her size, but not where it counted. Banking on the fact she probably stuffed her bra.

Hazel eyes bore into mine.

The girls noticed.

Sassy tapped my wrist with the file again. "Don't let her bait you."

Squinting, I quipped, "I don't."

There were three, "Uh-huh's," after my comment.

Ignoring us, Cher began to dig through her purse, briskly following the receptionist. Using too much sweetener in her voice made the explanation she was giving the girl come across as gritty and phony. She must be late for her appointment and was attempting bribery to keep her spot.

All of the employees were required to enforce the Late by Ten guideline. Without notification, the customer must reschedule, especially if they were getting a perm, color, or extensions. By the biblical book on salon rules, she was going to be forced to reschedule. *Yay, I'm saved.*

We all leaned over into the aisle to get a glimpse of whom she was talking too.

It appeared as though Ester was Cher's hairstylist or at least from what I could make out she was scheduled to be. I felt sorry for the petite, sweet, and perky woman. I never heard her utter a swear word or lose her temper, with anyone.

I gave her full marks for dealing with such a wide range of divas, every day. Ester was an angel and an artist when it came to hair care and styling. I scheduled time with her tomorrow at one for a wash and styling, and Fern squeezed in her appointment right after mine. We worked it out so I had a way to get here.

From Cher's tone and Ester's posture, things were about to take a turn for the worse.

"I'm sorry Cher, but you are twenty-two minutes late. You will have to reschedule. You know it's the policy."

"Look, I can't reschedule. The dance is tomorrow night and you are booked. I need my color refreshed, and the roots touched up. It's not going to take as long as a normal whole head color. At least touch up the roots and trim my layers a half-inch." Cher pulled her cell out and dropped her purse as if she had won the argument.

Ester's grip on her hand mirror turned white. "Cher, you have to reschedule."

"No, because the way I see it. You are taking up more of my time whining about applying a few swipes of color and ten minutes worth of cutting. You could have already been mixing it by now." She paid no attention to Ester's expression and kept her eyes on the screen, texting.

Realizing she wasn't going to get Cher out of the chair without a crowbar, Ester quietly set the mirror down and pulled out a smock. Walking behind Cher, she glanced in our direction. We leisurely removed ourselves from the awkward situation.

Sassy opened her mouth to comment when the plastic smock Ester held made an air snapping crack.

Cher squeaked.

The thump we heard immediately following—well one could only imagine, and we almost peed ourselves from laughter.

CHAPTER TWO

$\mathcal{E}$very time I raised my paper cup of vanilla coffee, I admired my cousin's one-inch nail masterpieces. Silver sparkled through the blue lacework she had taken an extra thirty minutes to freehand. I didn't even mind paying her the original thirty for the manicure, five for the additional detail, which I believed was not enough, so I gave her a twenty-dollar tip to show my appreciation.

I picked up the cup again when Fern cleared her throat. "You know, you are going to end up running to the bathroom every ten minutes the way you keep sipping your drink."

Flashing my polished nails at her, she giggled.

Deep in thought, Brie fiddled with her cardboard coaster as she sipped her hot chocolate. I assumed she was pouting since Fern sided with me on changing our plans from going to the movies, to hanging out at the Buzz. Only Fern and I needed our daily fix of caffeine, and the movies didn't serve coffee.

Britney held up her fingers to the light and sighed. "I'm

rethinking the color. My dress is hunter green, and my accessories are gold, but gold tipped nails. Do you think it's too much?"

"No, not at all. If you had painted the whole nail, then yes, it would be too much in my opinion." I set my cup down and grabbed her hand to assess my cousin's work. "I think it is elegant. What clutch did you decide on?"

"The small gold one, with the magnetic bow closure, it fits nicely in my palm. Keith is driving, so I'm only taking my house key, license, money, lipstick, finishing powder, cell…"

Fern spoke into her cup, "…And the kitchen sink."

Brie took her hand out of mine, extended it, then flipped up the middle three fingers at Fern. "Read between the lines."

I pinched her chin playfully to look at me and also to defuse the potential kitten fight. "What about the dark green clutch at Claire's? I think it would bring out the hint of gold in your nails and tone down the dipped in gold feel. Your shoes are gold too, right?"

She slipped through her teeth a breathless, "Yes."

Pushing the chair's metal legs over the tiles, Fern popped out of her seat. Clutching her coffee, she ran for the front door. The door buzzed as a man pushed on the handle. Practically knocking over the elderly couple trying to come in for their nightly fix, she chirped an apology but never stopped her momentum.

Britney blinked, then looked at me. "What did I say?"

Craning my neck to the side, I saw what burned her butt, Wade. He was with a few of his friends, who seemed to be giving him a hard time while the couple tried to talk. Wade, at first seemed shocked to see his girlfriend, but his demeanor shifted as though he was hiding something.

Brie followed my stare. "Oh, her jock alarm went off."

"Hey, Wade is all right. He is a lot better than her last few conquests."

We watched Fern through the winter characters painted on the window. Hopping from side to side trying to retrieve what Wade was keeping from her.

Britney turned in her chair to face me at the same time she picked up her drink. "You know, for all the teasing we do to each other, I wouldn't want to find myself on her bad side. M80's may be small but to have one go off next to you can deliver some damage. Not to mention you can hear the percussion five blocks away."

"Yeah, but would you rather have two dull sparklers or one M80 and one fizzle on a stick?" I bent over to get my wallet.

"Fizzle on a stick? Juslynn, if we weren't in public, I would punch your arm. Since when do you describe yourself as dull?"

I checked on Fern. They were laughing, and Wade's friends were standing closer to the electronic store, pointing at things in the window. "I don't know."

"What are you doing?"

"Looking for the shoe receipt."

"So, are you thinking about what Sassy said?"

Flipping through the pockets, I flashed a disappointed, flat-line smile. "No, I thought since Carter is taller than Peter, I need more height."

"Are you crazy? I know you like to feel tall but adding another inch, you are asking for trouble. And you know if I'm telling you that, you might want to forego the foot fashion for one night. Besides, I don't think Carter is going to be looking at your feet." She arched a perfect penciled eyebrow at me.

"Right. We'll talk about the next test in English, who I

think will win the Super Bowl this year, or who he wants to take to senior prom. Which is totally fine, I mean what else do best friends talk about?" My fingers kept folding and unfolding the receipts. "I know it's in here."

"Are you sure? I mean why go through the trouble if you'll be sitting at a table, drinking the school's nasty punch, and talking about Mr. Gregson's last assignment."

The door buzzed and I caught sight of a bouncy red-head meandering in our direction. Fern plopped down in the chair with a wide grin. Clutching her cup to help contain her excitement, it indented a little under bent fingers.

Brie acknowledged Fern first. "What's bake'n cupcake?"

"You are not going to believe this. Wade rented a stretch limo. It can fit all six of us. What do ya say? It will be fun."

I tried to match her excitement, but the truth was the only alone time Carter, and I would have, would be the drive. Instead of commenting, I waited for Britney to say something.

She shrugged. "Sure. It sounds roomy, in a cozy kind of way. Keith will be happy. He hates driving in the slush, and if he gets another ticket, he'll lose his wheels. We'll have nowhere to make out if that happens."

I punched her. *"Brie."*

"What? It's true. So, do you think Carter will want to ride with us misfits?"

"You make it seem as though he looks down on you. He is my male best friend, and I consider him a misfit too. Yeah, I'll talk to him. I'm sure it will be fine and fun."

My eyes wandered over to my hyper friend. "Yes, I'm sure he'll be cool with it. Where are we meeting, so the limo driver doesn't use Wade's time block from collecting everyone before the dance?"

"My house. Be there at four, and we'll get ready together."

The elderly man tapped me on the shoulder. "Miss, I believe you dropped something."

Following his shaky finger to the receipt between my feet, printed in bold, Shoe Box. "Thank you, sir."

See, fate stepped in. I was going to exchange my shoes tomorrow right after my hair appointment.

 used the back door so I wouldn't interrupt date night. My dad and Karia made it a point to always have time together on Saturday nights. I thought it was funny because my mom liked Dad's spontaneous nature; whereas Karia preferred order. She was perfect for the family business.

Down the hall, I heard the rattle of empty glasses clicking together, along with two sets of muffled steps toward the kitchen. There was no point in hiding, so I reached for a cup and a K-Cup of gingerbread flavored coffee, and then headed over to the sink. Their laughter grew louder as they came around the corner.

"Oops. We've been caught." Dad handed the wine glasses to Karia as he sidestepped from behind her to hug me. They were giddy from either the wine, each other, or both. Removing myself from my dad's half hug, I thought the answer was clear.

"Don't worry I won't report you, this time. At least you both have your clothes on."

Karia blushed but took the jab on the chin as she rinsed

the glassware in the sink. Dad came up behind her and kissed the back of her head.

From the sink, Karia abruptly turned off the water, and then playfully pushed my dad back to give her some space. "Juslynn, you okay?"

Involuntarily, my shoulders shrugged. I checked the brewer and realized I hadn't filled it yet. *Perfect.*

"Baby, what's wrong? Did you have a fight with the girls?"

Ugh! Was it some unwritten rule when I didn't answer them immediately something negative must have happened?

"No, no fight. As a matter of fact, it's just the opposite." Using a sarcastic, English accent, I said, "We had a superb time. Sassy did a flawless job—"

"She did? Let me see." Karia rushed forward to inspect my hands. Dad turned back to the dish drainer and started drying the glasses. My step-mother picked up my hand from the counter and studied the detail.

"Wow, this is awesome work. Is this what your dress looks like? I'm sorry I didn't get to go with you to pick one out."

The aroma from my coffee caused a wave of my past to crash over me.

Mom was sitting on the floor, right in front of me, next to the ottoman. Her silver etched tray, handed down from her grandmother, was arranged with Santa's cookies, sliced gingerbread, cocoa, and her special coffee cup.

I was eleven, and we were arranging our gifts under the family's angel tree. It was our tradition after they broke the news to me how Santa's story originated. Mom and I stuffed Dad's stocking. Little wrapped gifts and a special handmade gift from me went into the navy and gold sock.

The memory of her opening boxes of ornaments and handing me crystal angels, clay painted wings, which I made her in first grade.

Bulbs decorated with pictures of places in the clouds. There was one, that was her favorite. It looked like someone had torn a piece of the night sky and trapped it inside. A few tiny dots of light twinkled, and the darkness swirled as if there was a breeze that moved the moonlight-laced clouds. She would always stare at it longingly until a tear would trail down her cheek. Then she would hang it and pull me into a hug and whisper, "It was all worth it." I always meant to ask her, "what was?" But, after she got sick, the question faded into the moment I locked within my heart.

The ache from missing her blossomed inside and my back muscles tensed, probably from fighting the urge to cry. *I could really use your advice right now Mom, I thought.* She would have understood my emotional pros and cons for Carter. Mom had a knack for cracking the hard emotional-repelling shell I used to protect myself.

Taking a long blink, I watched her smile at me. This place in the back of my mind was my haven, and where I ran back to, to feel safe. A puff of warm air flowed over my hair. A kiss followed. Someone sighed against my ear from behind, as strong hands fell on my shoulders. Dave guided me back to reality before I decided to stay in the memory with my mom.

I blinked.

More tears ran down my face.

Absentmindedly, I rubbed my cheek and fought the reflex to sniff. *When did I start crying?*

Scanning the room for Karia, I noticed she had left to give me some time with my dad. She was used to my fadeout episodes and understood when they happened; it was something she couldn't help with. Dealing with our past was solely Dave's and mine to handle.

He turned me around for a hug. It was then I realized my body was trembling. We stayed quiet for a few minutes. Both of us, unsure who needed to break the room's silence.

Dad went first. "*Shhh*. I know J-baby, I know. Believe me; I miss her too."

I pulled back and looked down the hallway. "You do?"

His face went from concern to hurt. "Juslynn, it took me a long time to breathe. Even longer, to relearn how to live again."

Guilt made my voice small. "I know."

"Please, understand the love I hold for Cerena will never fade."

"I know."

"I love Karia too, but in a different way."

Folding my arms, I leaned back against the counter. "Dad, I just wish I could talk to her."

He cleared his throat. "Is it something I can help you with?"

My head slightly swayed.

"Is it something leaning toward female issues?"

I shrugged.

In a panic, Dave yelled, "Karia!"

My eyes flew open as I assessed the room. Nothing was on fire or flooding. The kitchen seemed fine.

In the archway, my step-mom and Spaz came skidding to a halt; Karia in her socks and Spaz on his butt. "Does Juslynn need the Heimlich?" Controlled fear paralyzed her face as Spaz barked. Her arms fell to her sides, waiting for instructions from my dad. "What's wrong?"

He averted his eyes while using a side up and down motion with his hand. "She is all yours."

"Wait, what?" We both blurted.

Then it hit me why the one male in my life was in a panic. I hadn't even come out of the batting box, and he was thinking I needed the female version of how the birds and the bees played baseball. Wounded pride colored my cheeks as liquid shame tried to cool them down. I was a jumbled mess and briefly wondered how my dad would have handled it if I told him Carter and I were as close as he assumed.

With an exasperated *tsk*, I turned to grab my lukewarm coffee. "Never mind. It's nothing. Come, Spaz."

Karia must have caught on to what he had insinuated because there was a calculated hesitation before she responded. "Juslynn, I'm not sure what's happened, but if you need to talk?"

"No, it's okay." I waved my free hand at them as I turned away. I didn't want her to see my face and know. Women have that intuition, like a shark's ability to detect a drop of blood. Instead, I used the blade of honesty. "And to put your mind at ease Dad, I'm not having sex, nor do I see it happening in my future. Thanks for assuming the worst."

Dave's throat strained when he started with, "Juslynn, I thought…" the apology that was about to happen was all the confirmation I needed.

Walking out of the room and hustling my butt upstairs was my way of protecting both of us. The problem with using honesty to wound, it works as a double-edged sword. I had to leave before our emotions bled out.

CHAPTER FOUR

Desperately in need of venting, I called Britney.

"No, he didn't?" She gasped.

"I'm so embarrassed." Rolling to the middle of my bed, I kicked my legs up onto the cherry wood headboard. We had been talking for the past forty minutes.

"I know you don't talk about your mom much but if you need me, you know I'm one button away. What number am I again?" Brie snickered right after asking.

"One."

"I'm sorry, I didn't quite hear you. What number?" I could tell she was smiling as she spoke.

"You're one, Brie. And Carter is two; my dad is three, Fern is four, Karia is five."

"You are belittling my importance here. You said I'm number one in your life."

Laughing, I said, "Alphabetically, cording to the program setting on my cell, yes."

"See, I'm first in your life."

"I could use last names."

"Ouch."

"Hey, thanks for the talk, Britney. I'm not sure why my brain decided that was the best time to open the door to one of my memories of her."

"It happens. But, I'm not going to pretend to understand what you are going through. I can listen, though, and if not me, I'm sure Carter would."

Hearing his name made my pulse spike. "Yeah, I'm sure he would too." *...as a friend.* My brain added to the sentence.

"Well, are you all right? If so, I'm heading to bed. My eyes are going to be bloodshot tomorrow if I don't get at least six hours."

"Yes, I'm fine. Thanks for making me laugh. I needed it. See you tomorrow."

"Night, Just."

"See ya, Brie."

The call disconnected, and I watched the dorky picture of us squeezing each other's cheeks dissolve to my screen saver. Thirty seconds later, it went into rest mode, leaving me and my subconscious alone to wander around in the dark. My mom's reassuring smile flashed from the back of my eyelids. It confused me as to why I was missing her so gravely. She had left us six years ago. I figured, by now, it should be getting easier for me; instead, I was finding it harder to move forward without her guidance.

Amazed by how fragile our lives were, I drifted to the day our world changed. One minute, the three of us were having fun washing the car, enjoying the sunny summer day. The next, a gust of wind barreled down our street, and it had become overcast. There was a booming outcry of my mom's name. Hands pushed me down, and I smacked the side of my head on the driveway. When I landed, I saw my mom on the ground from under the vehicle, facing me. Holding her stomach, she began to mouth something at me when a flicker of golden light lit from behind her pupils. It was so fast. I wasn't sure if what I saw were stars from hitting my head. I averted my gaze for half a second, to blink the stars away and when I looked back, I was met with a vacant expression.

Time ceased for me, and I don't remember when I realized I was in Dave's truck. We were following the ambulance to the hospital. Even at twelve, I knew from the way Dave held his posture as the silence grew between us, it was severe.

Dad sat me down in the waiting room reassuring me it would be fine. Then he disappeared through the emergency doors. I lost both parents that day; my mom to a brain aneurysm, and my dad to an imploding broken heart.

It took him three years to climb out of his black hole and back to me.

One morning he had come flying downstairs, pulled me out of the kitchen chair, causing me to drop my spoon of Lucky Charms. He held me like he was trying to make up for the last three years. It was like a light had turned back on behind his eyes.

Pulling back, he moved my hair and stared as if seeing me for the first time since my mother's death. There was something cryptic with his actions, as he whispered, "I don't know what I would do if I lost you to them too."

The memory smacked me awake. I had forgotten all about that day. Rubbing the grit from my eyes, I sighed. The room was cloaked in darkness, and I had fallen asleep in my clothes.

Stumbling to the bathroom, I clicked on the light, then closed my eyes until the harsh stinging subsided. After finishing my nightly routine, I went over what my brain had recalled. I was confident Dad had said, "…if I lost you to them."

Now, who was them?

CHAPTER FIVE

Sunday, December 18th, 2016.

"*B*ring Me to Life," by Evanescence, blared from the cell. It was on the fourth line when I snatched it off the nightstand. *Carter better have a good reason to be calling at this hour.* I knew it was his ringtone, but sleep was clogging my actions. Without thinking, I swiped the screen, then tried to moisten the cotton coating my tongue.

Groaning into the receiver, I managed one word. "Mmm. Morning." A yawn followed. The scent of warm caffeine drifted through the ceiling vent. Karia must be awake. *Coffee, I needed coffee.*

His raspy laughter sent a cascade of goosebumps down my neck, back and arms. In a dreamlike state, I pictured him lying in bed and wondered if he had just woken before calling me. My breath hitched, and my free hand cupped over my mouth, so I didn't huff into the mic.

Bolting upright, I blurted, "Carter?"

"Juslynn, I figured you would be up by now."

"What? Why?" I glanced at my docking system. Shocked, as I read 9:41 a.m. An "Oh," escaped, after falling back onto my pillow and closed my eyes to fight against the dizzies.

"So, what time would you like me to pick you up?" His question had a hint of amusement.

False start adrenaline spent, another yawn crept up on me, and I used the extra intake of air to slow my pulse rate. "I'm sorry, I meant to call you last night. There's a slight change in transportation if you are okay with it."

"What? You're driving?"

"No, Fern bumped into Wade yesterday. He rented a stretch limo."

"Oh, yeah?" His question was distant.

I rolled onto my side and propped a pillow between my neck and shoulder. "Wade invited us to ride with them. Is that okay with you?"

I heard the movement of sheets and a creak from a mattress spring. At the same time, Carter mumbled, but I couldn't quite catch what he had said. My brain only processed a few words like, never, when, alone, need, and talk.

Pressing the earpiece closer, I said, "What was that?"

Carter cleared his throat and somberly altered his response. "Umm, yeah, sure. If that is what you want to do."

"Well, we were kind of last minute and haven't really discussed what we were doing." I started to notice what Brie was implying about Carter. There was a distinct kind of distance between him and the rest of our friends. Then I became hyperaware that Carter never did anything with our click of friends alone, it was always if I was going, or if I had made plans with them and assumed he wanted to be included.

As I was going to confront him about it, he jumped in with, "Juslynn, it's fine. What time do I have to be at Wade's? Where are we picking the three of you up at, your house?" He seemed irritated.

"What makes you think Britney and Keith are coming with us?"

Carter was silent.

"We are getting ready at Fern's house. I'm supposed to be there around four." The tension pull between us reminded me of taffy as it cooled. *Was our bond stretched to the point of breaking?* Worried, I may have made him uncomfortable, I added, "Are you sure this is okay?"

His husky whisper sent chills down my neck. "I'm not looking for trouble is all."

"Why would you think that? It will be fun." My chipper reply faltered.

"Keith and Peter are tight." He stated flatly, but then he became hesitant. "I don't want Peter thinking I'm stealing his girl."

Maybe this was the attitude Britney was talking about?

His presumption sent me on the defense. "Umm, first off, Peter and I are not a couple. I am not *his* girl. We were going to prom together. Second, why would that bother you? It's not as if we are going as a couple. Your date fell through too, and I was a convenient substitute."

An audible sigh shot through the mic to hit me square in the chest.

I swallowed hard. "Carter, were you taking me as a–"

"You need to get up, Short-Stuff. I'll call Wade. Don't forget the rose to put between your teeth when we dance. See you tonight." Briskly he hung up before I could respond.

"Well, bye then!" I barked at the blank screen. Disgusted with his short jab, I dropped the cell on the bed. The crisp cut off ignited a new string of questions. The main one that concerned me the most was, *is this a date or not?*

CHAPTER SIX

We zipped through the drive-thru at the Buzz. Thank goodness Fern had the same caffeine dependency as me. While I told her the short version of my night with Dave and Karia, she abruptly decided to treat me to a vanilla coffee before planning our afternoon.

Walking into the salon, the level of estrogen slammed into us. For a brief moment, the zing of excitement and chatter made me smile. Girls were gossiping about their dates, where they were going for dinner, and who might be leaving with the crown.

Fern looped her arm through mine. "Honestly, I dreamt last night, Wade and I were crowned."

Stunned, I turned to face her. "Really? Can I ask you something?"

"Sure."

"How do you feel about Wade?"

She dropped her arm and narrowed her gaze. "I like him. Why?"

"I don't know. You seem different around him."

"Different?"

"He doesn't hide the fact that he cares for you. I was wondering if you felt more for him than like."

Smacking her thigh in nervous repetition, Fern had a deep crease in the middle of her forehead. I must have struck a nerve. A wet sheen appeared over both eyes. When she spoke, I had to strain to hear her. "I don't want to jinx it."

"What are you saying? Are you in love with him?"

She spoke through pursed lips. "I don't want to jinx it."

"Fern, I like Wade. I think you two make an awesome couple."

"Do you?" she said with such vulnerability, it crushed my heart.

"Yes, I do. Now let's go get you prettified and knock the socks off of him."

The smile she beamed at me could have lightened a path at midnight with no moon.

Ester stood on her stool, in front of her mirror with a Cheshire grin, watching us from the reflective surface as she finished wiping down the mirror.

Fern and I laughed as we approached the chair.

Ester jumped down with the grace of a cat and spun the chair around, to show a long stem blue rose encircled with baby's breath and wrapped in silver foil. There was a card next to it.

Both of us pointed at each other with a shocked O face. The beautician picked up the card and flipped it over.

Fern grabbed my arm in a vice grip. "It's to you!" She shouted.

There was a crashing wave in between my ears. When I took the card from Ester, my heart was pounding.

Upon opening the envelope, I took the card out. Two characters were dancing on the front, above them was written in a flourishing script, Just for You. Holding my breath, I read the message inside.

Bear with me, for I can't rhyme nor keep time
And with that in mind… here I go.

An Invitation to Dance.
Sometimes my words are thorns and I
Can't always express what I mean clearly.
But let me be the first to say and
Ask you in the correct way,
Will you go to the Snow Flurry Dance with me?

I hope you'll say yes,
Because you already have the dress.
And I don't want to return my tux,
Because they don't give refunds.

Carter

My mouth fell open at the same time that pesky little voice inside my head whispered, *but if you defrost the frozen milk, what will happen if it spills this time?*

CHAPTER SEVEN

Fern tried to talk me out of stopping at the Shoe Box, but once my mind is made up, I became stubborn. I would have walked from her house and back if I had too. And that was the excuse I gave her if she didn't give me fifteen minutes to exchange and try on.

"I promise," I started to say through the open door, "fifteen minutes tops."

She moaned. "Okay, but I don't want to move around too much with this twisted bun. It's heavy, and I'm afraid of the earth's gravitational pull; I can feel it." Fern checked the time on the dash. "Fifteen minutes or you are walking to my house."

Not thinking, I shut the door without collecting my things. Blowing a stray curl from my face, I reached in for my purse and shoe bag. Fern handed them to me, and the shoes made a sliding noise as I pulled the box through the window. The glass window started to rise, and I noticed Fern's finger on the button.

I mouthed, "Jerk."

She laughed.

When I dashed into the shoe store, the aroma of new shoes hit me. I loved the smell. Both feet came to a halt when I saw the line at the counter had six people in it. I bypassed it and went to see if the ones I wanted were there. Walking four rows over, muttering "excuse me" nine times, I started to think the shoes were gone. The place was wall to wall with people shopping for the holidays. In the back of my head, I heard Fern's voice in my head, "fifteen minutes."

"Yeah, right. Fifteen minutes," I said to myself.

"What?" came from behind me.

It was Cher.

"Marvelous," I said, internally dripping with disdain.

With tongue in cheek, I slowly turned around; damning myself for even acknowledging her.

I screwed on my plastic smile. "Nothing. I was reminding myself of something."

She grinned, leaning against the shoe rack. Then I cringed, she wasn't buying shoes. Her name tag read HELLO MY NAME IS… I wanted to fill in the blank using a red sharpie with something other than CHER.

"Talking to yourself, that's cute. Be careful not to answer; it's how crazy starts."

"You would know." My quip caused a self-gratifying half smirk, even though, part of me knew the comment was in poor taste.

It made sense now why she was so insistent with Ester yesterday. She had to work before the dance. Then I wondered why she just didn't explain that to the beautician. Then it dawned on me, *Cher's working?*

"Listen," she had started to raise her voice, but the manager locked in on her tone and walked over.

The manager faced me. "Is everything okay?"

I may not like Cher, but I wasn't going to get her fired, even if she wasn't customer friendly at the moment.

Maybe I'll have a little fun, and flashed a wicked smile.

Cher stiffened.

Facing the manager, I glanced at her nametag, Katie. Then I gushed out with, "No, no, everything is peachy-keen. Cher here was telling me about the clearance choices. And let me say, I love coming here." *Not a lie.* "The customer service is like butter on toast. She has been so warm and friendly." *Complete lie.* I justified it, for my snide crazy comment. It was the least I could do.

Cher held her mouth open, taking two side steps to stand behind her boss. Never taking her eyes off of me, then mouthed the word why.

Katie turned abruptly toward Cher causing her to blink away the shocked expression. Next, her boss said, "Keep up the good work. I'll put this complement into your file. Great job." She started to walk away then spun around with her finger up. "I know you're going to the dance tonight. You can clock out fifteen minutes early if you want."

That was fate reminding me I was pressed for time as well.

Not even acknowledging Cher, I nodded at the manager and quickly said, "Thanks for the reminder." Turning on a heel, I then mini shuffled down the aisle.

Setting my sights on the eight and a half sign I kicked myself mentally for losing focus on my shoe mission. When I reached the dress shoes, I pulled out my cell. I had eight minutes left.

Another curl came loose and was bouncing next to my right eye. Repeatedly, I kept blowing the slight nuisance away while carefully scanning each open-faced box. Then I saw them. The sparkle from these peep-toe, sling-backs, with the four-inch heel, made me smile. I was in fashion love; they were perfect for my dress and would solve our height difference.

Carter would notice me in these, even if it killed me. I vowed to myself.

Cradling the box, I checked inside each shoe for the size and to check for scuffs on the heels. Pleased, I ambled toward the register. It was unfortunate that there wasn't enough time for me to try them on, but beauty did hurt sometimes, and I would place the bet they would fit.

Just my luck, there were eight people in line. There was a thirty-something woman at the counter complaining about two different sizes in the box to the cashier. She kept emphasizing for someone to find her the right size.

Sulking, I didn't want to glance at the time again. If this line didn't start moving, I was going to be walking.

Two girls rushed in shaking the snow out of their hair.

Correction, I was going to be walking to Fern's in the snow.

Another employee I hadn't recognized came from the back of the store. Turned on the second register and said, "If you have an exchange, I'll take you over here."

No one moved.

With a flood of relief, I sent a small, *thank you,* into the universe. Time must be on my side after all.

CHAPTER EIGHT

A damp makeup cloth moved over my face in angry succession. Britney was upset with Keith but hadn't disclosed to us why. My nerves were so frayed that Brie said I was suffering from clown-face. I hated clowns. No, rephrase that, I was scared to death of clowns. The fact Britney wouldn't let me see myself said a lot.

Frustrated, I spoke between swishes of the cloth. "Hey. I'm not a car, stop trying to buff out my imperfections."

She straightened, holding the used sheet. "Do you want me to spackle it on or do you want it to appear flawless?"

Reapplied makeup would make my skin appear cakey, I knew this. My shoulders rolled forward. "Okay, I understand, but you are taking off my eyebrows."

With force, she tossed the cloth in the trash. *Yup, something was bugging her.*

Fern came bouncing in, on bare feet, holding the front of her dress. Britney already attacked her face; she glowed like a Disney princess. Fern's actions helped defuse the mood in the bathroom. I giggled.

"I'm in need of assistance." She danced from side to side, then spun to show the open zipper. "Up, please."

Without even really looking, Brie clasped the zipper. I blinked. *Yup, missed it.* Fern was walking out of the room.

"How do you do that and not catch skin?"

She shrugged.

"Britney, what's wrong? The night will be ruined for all of us if you keep acting this way. Plus," I took her hands in mine while keeping eye contact, "it's our last winter dance we'll attend as seniors. This should be memorable, not regrettable."

"I know," she said, through tight, mauve-painted lips. "It's me; it's always me. Keith even stated, 'It's always my fault.'" Tear soaked lashes fluttered, as she tried to fight the drops from ruining her mascara. With a note of despair, she asked, "But, is it always me?"

Couple drama isn't what we needed tonight. I wanted to help, not make things worse, and I wasn't sure how to explain without ripping the Band-Aid off. Most girls were 'me-me's' sometimes. I knew this, and we all suffer from it especially when defending ourselves. Recently, I was struggling with the same internal symptoms. The difference was that I was selfishly fighting against my feelings. But the fear of Carter finding out… I briefly had a daymare, envisioning his negative reaction to my confession. I broke my gaze from hers so she wouldn't see my pain. I understood loneliness, and Britney was worried Keith might be right and she would end up alone tonight.

Taking a cleansing breath, I pushed my dumb fears aside. First, I needed to find out why she felt this way. "Before you take out your hurt and anger on my face with too much eyeliner and make me EMO, tell me what happened."

She released my hands and sank to the floor in her top

half-slip and sheer nylons. Mounts of curls made her resemble a wounded lioness. *Tread with care*, I thought.

"Earlier today Keith took me out to lunch. He said that he needed to ask me a question."

My breathing stopped, but I used a hand gesture for her to continue.

"He took me to Gary's Steakhouse, the one off of Main St."

"And?"

Fern crossed the bathroom's threshold and saw Brie on the floor. "What did you do to her?"

Britney gave a sidelong glance at Fern.

"What?"

Impatiently, I pointed to the tub, for her to sit down.

Brie rocked forward onto her toes and walked out of the room.

I mumbled under my breath, but loud enough to be heard. "Terrific timing, Fern, she was just about to tell me what was bugging her."

She sat with a *tsk*. "Like that's my fault. I'm not a mind reader. I knew she was mad, but I didn't think it was all that serious."

Britney clutched her purse as she walked back into the room. When she sat back down in front of us, she upended it. All the contents fell to the floor. There was a wine-colored jewelry box tumbling down the pile of stuff. It stopped in the middle of the floor.

Sighing she reached for it. A crease appeared in between her eyebrows, as she stared at the box. Three seconds later, her thumb pressed the clasp, the lid opened. A gold promise ring, with a diamond in the middle of the heart, glittered in the bathroom light.

Fern and I froze.

"He asked me to wait for him. Keith wants to marry me in the future. Marry. Me." Her eyes filled with tears.

"This is why you are mad?" Fern's question hung in the air like a heavy raincloud full of disappointment.

"Yes. We are eighteen. Going to college. Beginning our lives outside of Bothell, and he wants me to wait? What if he changes his mind in a year or two?"

Unsure, I asked, "So, he asked you to wait for him to ask you officially?"

"In a way, yeah. So, I can't say, I'm engaged. It's a promise." She looked at the ring in disgust. "I told him if he really wanted me, he would have proposed, not leave me with the promise of one. How can I take this seriously; this keeps the door wide open for both of us." She closed the lid with a snap and sniffed. Worry marred her face; she was trying really hard not to cry. "I should have brought my waterproof mascara."

Fern and I chuckled to lighten the mood.

Buckling my legs under the stool, I slipped to the floor on my knees and wrapped both arms around her shoulders. "Britney, it may not be what you wanted to hear exactly, but look at it this way, he just expressed out loud, that he promises to be there. To be your everything. Only you."

Brie studied the ring box. "But, it leaves so much room to stray away from each other. Then he can say, 'Well, it was only a promise.' Then what do I do?"

"Oh, Britney." Fern landed on her knees with a thump. Her dress was too tight for her to sit on the floor with us. Still, she managed to add in her hug on top of mine. "Do you realize how many people get engaged and then break it off? An engagement ring doesn't protect you from the dark side of love either. If you believe in each other, you fight for it."

With some enthusiasm, I added my two cents. "You are very fortunate to have someone who wants to promise you his future. In a way–he did propose," In my chest, the ache to be wanted was back. I could taste the film of jealousy on the back of my tongue.

Fern grabbed Britney's face. It was a dangerous move since Brie had already made-up her face. But the action worked, she had her attention. "I happen to know; Keith's family holds to their heritage. A promise ring is a huge deal. He did ask you to marry him, in the future." Shaking her fiery hair, she took a big intake of air. "You're getting married!"

Britney jolted from Fern's outburst.

Wincing, I internally rolled up my negative emotions and jumped to my knees to match Fern's excitement. "You're getting married!"

We fell on top of one another in the middle of the bathroom. I rolled off of Brie and grabbed her hand. "See, this is what I was talking about. We just turned regret into a happy memory. Now, can you finish my makeup without bruising my face?"

Fern rolled away, resembling a mermaid out of the water, trying to stand up on her fins. "Yes, we need to hurry up." She tugged down the skirt and smoothed it out. "They will be here in thirty minutes."

We yelped, scattered and finished primping, painting, and dressing.

In Fern's bedroom, I slipped my dress on, and Brie did her magic zip zipper pull. At the same time, I set the shoe box on the bed and flipped the lid off. Their gasps followed the *ta-da* moment.

Fern excused herself as Britney sat on the bed next to the box. "Those are gorgeous."

I sat on the other side of the box and pulled the crumpled tissue paper out of each shoe. Laughing, I slipped my right foot in and buckled it. I repeated the motions with my left foot. The sparkle made me fashion-drunk.

Pointing my toes, Brie whistled.

Fern walked in with three bottles of water, slowing her pace to a stop as if she was seeing me for the first time. My friend's face twisted with concern. I was about two inches taller than them.

My brow set in a defiance scowl. "What's wrong?"

Fern cleared her throat. "They are pretty." Then, took a sip of water.

Hands on my hips, I felt the bite of several sequins under my fingers. "That's it? That's why your face looks like someone just told you your dog died?"

A penciled eyebrow arched. "No, even pretty things can be deadly."

From across the bedroom, Britney spoke, "The guys are here. Wade wasn't kidding. The limo is huge. And..." She leaned against the window, squinted and faced the darkened sky.

I latched the clasp on my cape. "And, what?"

"It's snowing."

CHAPTER NINE

The doorbell rang, and Fern's mom yelled for her husband to get the door. Then a booming request for us to come down, drowned out Dave Kaye and Bing Crosby's musical skit in White Christmas. Fern's mother was baking and the fragrance of sugar cookies added to the warm and joyful sensation swirling in the air.

In a rush we gathered what we needed from the bed and bathroom, each of us did one more check in the bathroom mirror, an inspection spin, and then headed out. A French-manicured hand smacked my arm, stopping me from reaching the door.

"Ouch! Hey?"

"You're forgetting something." Fern gestured at the nightstand.

An overwhelming mixture of foolish and shyness made my stomach flip-flop. It was where I placed the blue rose and card from Carter right after we got back from running errands. In five toe-steps, I made it to the stand and grabbed the flower.

From my quick movement, the rebellious curl was back. I blew it from my eye. "Is it okay if I leave the card here?" Holding up and swinging the silver clutch for a visual. "I don't think it will fit in here."

She shrugged. "Sure, besides, I was going to ask you and Brie if you wanted to come back here later."

"Oh?" It caught me by surprise. I assumed we'd go our separate ways after. At least, that's what I was hoping, so I could have some time with my friend-date.

"So, do you? If the night goes bad, we can drown our woes with cookies and coffee." Her smile was inviting. *How could I say, no?*

Involuntarily, I shrugged. "Really? Bribing me? You had me at cookies." Pushing forward on my toes, I swooshed past my friend then turned to smack her playfully on the nose with the blue rose petals. "Thanks for this."

She raised her face to meet my gaze. "You are so tall in those. I can't believe how naturally you carry yourself. It's almost like you're walking on air."

"Thanks." Taking the compliment made me flush with pride.

But then, she added, "Juslynn, please don't forget you are walking on stilts." Keys jingled as Fern locked her bedroom door.

So much for the compliment, I thought.

Britney stopped at the top of the stairs and put her hand over the middle of her chest in a show of sappy sentiment.

A smirk grew on my face as I asked, "What?"

Gold nails flashed out to stop me from advancing and then motioned for Fern to come toward her.

A light pink smile formed, but the wrinkle in between Fern's eyes betrayed a hint of worry. Placing her bedroom key in the hunter green clutch with a snap, Fern timidly obeyed the girl beckoning from the stairs. Slightly tilting her head, afraid that gravity might magnetically pull her down by her hair, she hesitated. "What's up, Brie?"

Impatient, a blur of brown curls and arms lunged to pull the petite girl next to her. With a graceful trip and a hop, she stopped right next to Britney. Motionless, Fern followed Brie's gaze to the bottom floor.

Positioning myself behind Fern, I saw Wade at the foot of the stairs. He wore a black and red solid slim fit tuxedo, with matching accessories to Fern's dress. He held a bouquet of white lilies, her favorite, in one hand and the other behind his back. With a genuine *come to me*, smile; he encouraged Fern with a small motion with the flowers.

Excited for her, I went to place my hand on her shoulder and found nothing but air. Britney and I were left staring at each other. The only trace of Fern was the perfumed breeze.

Astonished, I gasped before asking, "How did she make it down to him so fast in that dress?"

She raised one shoulder. "I guess it's true."

"What?"

With an impish grin, said, "She must have sprouted wings."

Yeah, I heard love could do that, I thought.

We click-clacked down the stairs in unison.

Wade swung Fern several times and then planted a kiss on her cheek before gracefully slowing them down to a full stop.

She stumbled a bit. "You already made me lightheaded. Did you have to spin me too, you big oaf?" She held her stomach until her world realigned. Giggling, she playfully smacked his arm with her clutch.

Brie and I were mesmerized, watching the Hallmark scene unfold in front of everyone. Then a low whistle came from the corner by the front door. I could feel Keith's eyes on us. I gave Britney a nudge.

He held out a corsage. "I had them fashion it so you can wear it on your wrist or I can use this magnet. I know how you are with your clothes." Keith's bangs fell over one eye as he tilted his face to hide the slight blush forming on both cheeks. I was surprised to find that bashfulness could be charming.

Britney opened her small purse and pulled out the ring box. "I did some thinking, and I'm sorry." Her hand shook, she was nervous. The exhale I heard sparked my own sympathy pains for my friend. Finding her courage, she added, "I'm sorry for the way I acted today. I'm sorry for taking you for granted. Sometimes, I do make things about me, but if you know how I can be and are willing to promise me a future, then, if it's all right with you..." Her apology became meek.

Keith plucked the box from Britney's fingers and opened it. Pulling her left hand toward his chest, he sighed. "I wouldn't have asked you to stand beside me if I didn't believe you are the right girl to complete me." He realized we were all staring at them. "Since everyone's here; Britney, with this ring, I promise to ask for your hand in the future. Do you promise to wait for that day?"

Blurred with wet happiness for my friend, I glanced at Carter. His facial features hardened, and I couldn't tell if he was breathing. He was intently glaring at Keith and Brie. I swiveled my gaze from the happy couple and back. No, Britney. *Why?*

A breathless, "yes," slipped from her lips.

Keith slid the ring on as they kissed, sealing their vow.

Disappointed and confused by my best friend's actions, I dropped my head and sighed before joining the merriment.

We hooted and clapped, while Wade smacked Keith on the back and made marriage jokes. Carter surprised me when I saw him from my peripheral vision, approach and shake Keith's hand to congratulate him. Fern, Brie and I dried our happy tears as we hugged. Then I noticed Fern's parents were clapping too. Probably elated it wasn't their daughter we were congratulating.

A bloom of warmth traveled from chest to face, filling my cheeks with the same sensitivity. Smiling, I glanced where Carter was last. A twinge of panic made my breath hitch as I scanned the room for his presence.

Standing in the corner by the front door, his silhouette was backlit by the porch light streaming through the side window. Downcast eyes focused on the floor. The air around Carter projected *stay way*.

Concerned, I ignored the warning and found myself in front of him.

Leisurely, lifting his head, he momentarily stopped on the rose, before his eyes roamed over my dress until they found mine. Clenching his jaw, I wondered why he was trying so hard not to communicate. He hadn't even said, hi, to me. There was a growing void behind each of his blinks, and I fought between reaching out to him or smacking his shoulder.

Carter's mood didn't match the enthusiasm level of the room. Anger cranked up my internal voice as it started to second guess what our friendship meant to him. *Weren't these people his friends too? Why was he acting so closed off? Didn't he want to be here?* My grip on the flower tightened.

The protective nature for my friends threatened to push me away from Carter. *Maybe the girls were right, insinuating that he looked down on them.*

With several of my unanswered questions swirling around, he exhaled and moved the sheer curtain to stare out the window. *Wasn't he even going to acknowledge me? I was close enough to detect his toothpaste.*

Our moment was interrupted by a chilly sensation raising the hairs on the back of my neck and arms. The hush of a sentence penetrated my ears, like barely audible static. *"Jus-lynn, if you only knew,"* pressed against the back of my mind. I blinked several times. Carter's mouth was set in a frown.

Bewildered, I whispered, "What did you say?"

He whipped his head in my direction. "What?"

I leaned forward. "Didn't you just say something?"

Overcast, sea-blue eyes dove into my soul, and I shivered from the chilly intensity. He hesitated, while slowly shaking from side to side. "No. No, I didn't." Carter turned his attention back to whatever was beyond the glass.

The room's noise enveloping us vanished. All the adjectives I could muster dried to my tongue as my gaze coveted the male in front of me. The black tux hugged Carter's physique in ways I never dreamed. My eyes burned his features to memory, taking in the way the jacket defined his waist and broad shoulders. How the crisp white tux shirt seemed to mold over muscle. I followed the buttons to the collar, my breath caught.

It was blue, royal blue.

He had exchanged the accessories. I knew Cynthia's dress was Christmas red because we passed each other coming out of the dressing rooms the day I bought mine.

I bit my lower lip; allowing myself a guilty, slow-eyed glide to his face. Carter's dark hair was in a messy windblown style. There was a slight cut on his chin, possibly from shaving. Desire made my fingers twitch as I fought the urge to trace the skin next to the scar.

Completely unaware, I broke this new-found silence between us with a long exhale.

He mumbled, fogging the glass then gradually turned back to me.

Reason warred with my emotions. Reason screamed; *he is your best friend.* Emotions; purred, *titles could change.*

"Hey Short-Stuff, I see you got the flower." He unbuttoned the jacket and proceeded to search the inside pocket. It opened enough for me to notice the matching cummerbund.

I couldn't breathe. Lips slightly parted to intake some oxygen before I passed out quickly. He was intoxicating.

Carter's attention shifted to my mouth.

My jaw went slack. *Yes? Is he going too…*

A punch on his arm made us both jump. Keith smirked. "Hey, we better get going. The dance started almost twenty minutes ago."

Before I knew what was happening the girls' each took an arm and spun me toward Fern's parents. Several flashes went off. Then they told us to pose with our dates.

I started sweating under the mounds of curls.

Fern's mom told Carter and me to stand in the middle since I was tallest of the three girls. We staggered ourselves on an angle. The guys to the right; but standing behind us. We were in front and to the left.

Carter stood behind me, stiff with his arms at his sides.

Another flash went off.

Wade and Keith were leaning against their dates. It was a simple display of affection. Jealously twisted its way into my heart. White spots floated around the room. When I blinked, my lashes were damp.

Another flash.

One tear tried to escape, and I dabbed it before the mascara had a chance to smear. My growing doubts and Carter's walls were making the distance between us seem impassable. The only way, I would be able to keep him in my life was for us to remain friends. If I confessed, things would become awkward, especially if he didn't see me beyond the scope of a friend.

Yes, if I stopped dwelling on him, the romantic feelings would fade in time. I could forget, would forget, and then neither of us would end up hurting.

Fern's mom chided, "One more. Everyone say, 'Mistletoe.'"

Fingers lightly touched my hip; an electrical zap startled me, then the bite of current traveled down the length of my backside. Another hand slid around my waist to tug me backward. He masked a grunt as he closed the space between us. When the next static charge popped, it was painful, and I was positive it left a burn mark somewhere on my lower back, but he still held me.

Pressure similar as before pressed into my ear canals. Carter's breath fluttered against the back of my right ear. "Hurting, is a part of being human, right?"

Like an idiot, I turned stoic and pasted on a smile.

Some of us said Mistletoe.

Did he actually respond to my thoughts?

There was a flash.

Right after the shutter click, he took a step back.

I was alone again and the moment… was gone.

CHAPTER TEN

The wind caught my cape as I headed down the stone walkway. It fluttered softly in the breeze making me feel fictional, like a princess in a story.

I stole a glance in his direction; *and the prince?*

My prince was fictional too. He was my best friend, but now, we were both acting as though our parts in the story were altered. It didn't feel natural, and this scared me.

The limo driver came around the back and opened the door, holding out his hand to help us into the car. Then the driver bowed with a little more flourish than I thought was called for. He wore the standard cap and gloves, but the strange thing about him was the mirrored sunglasses. *Can we say, over dramatizing?*

The driver held out his starched white glove. "My Lady."

A bristle of hostility made me balk, and I almost slipped on the sidewalk.

Ignoring the unexplainable sensation, I commented through a tight smile. "Well, it seems we are getting the full treatment tonight?"

"It's all part of the service." He straightened and pulled his glasses down. A flicker of green appeared, then disappeared in the middle of his irises. Then using the same finger to push his glasses back into place, before his open hand reached for mine. "Yes, my lady, you're almost ready."

With a slight shake, to internally dismiss the driver's actions, I hesitated before asking, "What did you say?"

A low rumble diverted my attention, which within two blinks, Carter came from behind. "Is there something wrong here?"

The response was spoken with a fake smile. "I don't believe so, sir."

After the driver's response and Carter's domineering presence, it left me queasy.

Placing a hand on my stomach, I asked the driver again, "What did you say to me?"

He snatched my hand with a tad more force than I thought was needed. "Sorry, if you didn't hear me. I asked, 'If you were ready?'"

The rolling rumble intensified, almost like a dog refusing to give up his bone. When I leaned back, there was a vibration emanating from my date. As I turned to face him, the zap I felt made me stop and I sucked in the cold air too fast making my lungs quiver. *Was I his bone?* Referring to myself as dog food ruined my princess perception. I wasn't sure if there was a misunderstanding between the two of them. It was almost as though they knew each other.

Carter cleared his throat, but I was worried we might snap, crackle, and pop again if he touched me and I didn't want to sound like cereal. So, I allowed the driver to help me into the limo; muttering, "Thank you," when I positioned myself to sit down.

The driver tipped his hat and backed away giving Carter

about a five feet radius to enter. With half of his body outside the limo, they started to exchange words.

A harsh muffled tone came from the driver that I couldn't comprehend. It was as though he spoke in a foreign language. Upon hearing one of his sentences, I felt my core temperature rise a degree or two. Each second felt heavy as if time was slowing down and I turned to my friends who didn't seem phased at all by what was happening.

Carter spoke bluntly, and in the same language, which scared me a little since I had never known this side of him.

Then the conversation stopped.

All the heaviness vanished, and it was then that I noticed Carter sitting across from me next to Keith. The driver got in, closed the door and started the vehicle. Everyone was laughing and talking like nothing was out of the ordinary. Carter's lips pressed into a frown as he stared out the window with an uneasiness about him. Brie was showing off her ring to Fern. Wade and Keith were debating which hockey team would take the cup this year.

It was as if someone had clipped out five minutes of my life, and the conversation I had overheard was carried off into the inky blackness of night.

No one asked me about what had transpired between the driver and Carter, therefore, if I wanted to ask about it, none of them would remember.

But, I did.

CHAPTER ELEVEN

The December chill swirled around us long enough to kiss our cheeks to leave a slight burn. It stopped snowing by the time we arrived. The light dusting of ice flakes on the trees and grass left the perfect atmosphere for the Snow Flurry Dance.

Fashionably late, we headed for the steps leading to the gym. First was Wade and Fern, then Brie and Keith, Carter and I were last on the stairs. Everyone made small-chat about how long we wanted to stay, if we should go to the movies dressed up, or hang out at Wade's and order pizza.

Our conversation was getting livelier, but Carter remained closed lipped. He scanned the parking lot. His body language projected high alert bodyguard rather than an average guy escorting a girl to prom. The parking lot lights made his facial features appear edgier.

Consumed with the desire to touch his cheek, left me unaware when the breeze swept down the stairs and lifted my cape, tugging it back enough to knock me off balance. Then it curved under my right foot as I stepped onto the top step.

Shocked to find myself falling forward, I overcorrected and then panicked. Alarm lodged in my throat as I dropped the clutch. Instinctively, I grabbed for the railing.

Closing my eyes tightly as the cool air enveloped me.

"Ouch." I yelped as a jolt of current traveled across my back, hip and down my leg. A low grunt breathlessly brushed past my neck. I cussed at myself for wearing this stupid cape. Not only was it endangering my health, but it was full of static. The zaps Carter and I kept sharing was getting old. No wonder he didn't want to touch me.

Opening one eye, I found myself cradled in a pair of taut, strong arms. Carter had caught me before I had made a mess of things. Once he righted me, I found myself on the step above his. We were only inches from each other. The left side of his mouth twitched as his eyes dropped to my lips. The spike I felt within my heart made me wonder if it could beat faster without exploding. Where his hands held me turned hot.

Then a voice cut through my daydream. "As if that wasn't calculated. Juslynn's first fail for the night."

Cher.

In a quick flourish, Carter picked up my clutch and then urged me to keep moving before I said or did something to embarrass him, me, or my friends.

Since she fired the first shot, it wouldn't be right for me not to retaliate. I dragged my feet long enough to send her darts through my eyes and mouthed, *'Just wait.'* At the same time, a silver clutch blocked my view of her, and I turned my glare at Carter.

"It's amazing how human you can be. You shouldn't let the girl get under your skin. Anger taints the soul." He frowned and placed the purse in my hands and stepped around me to the entrance.

His comments stung, like an antidote to poison. This silent war between Cher and myself had gone on for years. Carter seemed disappointed, and it made me self-conscious as my gaze shifted to focus on my nemesis.

She laughed and leaned against her… I assumed, date. With Cher, you never knew. Come with one guy, dance with another, to leave with a different one altogether. She was a piece of work.

I followed behind the group like a scolded child. Keith opened the door and waited for everyone to enter. Brie stayed beside him while we entered the gym. A flood of voices followed by thumping music hit me in the chest, and I suddenly wanted to dance. Stunned, all six of us took in what the student council and graphic art's club created.

There was a multitude of different shaped snowflakes, light blue, white, and silver coated in glitter and hanging from the ceiling. A center strobe light spontaneously hit them, causing sparkles around the room, giving it a flurry effect. I was impressed.

A photo booth, with a red sleigh and props, was positioned to the left by the first set of exit doors. To the right, there were two sets of curtains hanging on either side of a table with a sign that read, "Tickets and Check-In." Another set of doors separated the ticket booth and the food tables. Beyond that was the punch fountain. The DJ's makeshift booth was set up at the back of the room facing the dance floor.

Some of the students volunteered as fill-ins for when the DJ needed a break. I didn't know the guy with the headphones on, but his face was familiar. I watched him punch a few buttons, and then "Rockin' Around the Christmas Tree" started to play.

Wade motioned for us to head to the check-in booth.

Carter gestured to follow while he pulled out two tickets. My foot tapped with the beat as I waited in line.

One of the girls on the other side of the table raised her voice. "Tickets?"

Carter leaned forward to hand them to her. She checked the numbers, hole punched the edge, then gave them back. He, in turn, handed one to me. "Just in case you need to step out for anything, you can get back in."

I nodded, putting the ticket in my silver clutch.

Leaning in, he cupped his hand so I could hear. "Do you want to check-in your cape and clutch?"

"The cape, yes."

He reached around to remove it as I unclasped the clip, his hands landing on mine. Every cell fired at once. The jolt made my knees weak and my head throb. If we didn't stop shocking each other, this night was going to be a disaster.

We found an empty table ten minutes later. Keith and Britney went to get drinks. Wade picked up Fern and ran on to the dance floor. Carter and I were where I thought we exactly would be, at the table.

He pulled my chair out and tucked me in, then pulled out the one on my right. Unbuttoning his jacket before he sat down, he looked as though he was going to say something. Then sighed, shook his head, and sat down next to me. I filled in our unspoken time together people watching. *Yeah, this is fun.*

Brie came back carrying three sodas, Wade with the same. She set them down and handed me a diet. Carter took a can from Wade and popped it.

I did a double take when I saw him chugging it. The corners of his eyes creased, as he continued to pull on the can. Finally, with a gasp-sigh, he set the empty can down.

Britney's eyes were wide, and Keith's gawk matched hers.

Carter looked at Keith. "Thanks, Man, I needed that."

He laughed. "I can see that. Do you need another one?"

"No, I'm good. Thanks."

Brie kept staring at him. I snapped at her to stop. She mouthed, "What was that all about?"

I shrugged, indicating no clue.

She turned to Keith and did a finger twirl then pointed to the dance floor.

He took her hand and off they went.

Glancing at Carter, I watched him pull on his collar. He seemed uncomfortable, and maybe even nervous.

I couldn't stand it anymore, I was going to suggest we leave, but the empty chair next to me already spoke volumes.

CHAPTER TWELVE

lone, I watched the couples' dance, laugh, and carry on together. I even saw the vice-principle twirling around with the eleventh-grade science teacher. Rejection plunged the blade even deeper.

Music thumped, but I wasn't paying attention to what was playing. Confusion replaced my date for tonight. It's what I get for putting my head in the mouth of *what if*.

Going over how I got here began to sweep me out to a sea of tears. First, Carter asking if I wanted to still go to the dance, even though our dates fell through. The tense wake-up call we had from this morning. The surprise he arranged for me at the salon. The glances he gave me. His reaction when we got our pictures taken. The weird, almost protective vibe he gave off to the limo driver. Catching me in midair, and drawing me in so close I could smell his toothpaste. And last on my countdown, leaving me without an excuse or even saying, "I'll be right back."

None of his actions made sense.

Blinking, I felt the first tear threaten to fall. I pried myself away from the table and made a beeline to the girls' bathroom. I slammed into the last stall and gave in to my emotions. I knew I was in love with him and obviously, the desire was one-sided.

The flood of misery overpowered every emotion I carried for him. Toying with the idea, if I could give all my wishing stars to the sun and watch every one of my thoughts of him evaporate, would the pain subside too. Then I could start anew and recreate a dreamless sky.

I used some tissue from the stall to dab my eyes and tried to calm the sobs from becoming hiccups. Carter's blue eyes appeared in my mind. I was hopeless; my first wish would be to recreate the sky with him.

The door to the bathroom opened and filled the room with an echo of drums and base. Once it closed, there was a click-clack of heels until they stopped in front of a sink. Water sprayed, and then I heard murmurs; the person was talking to themselves. It made me think about what Cher said earlier.

When I ran in, I didn't even think to see if anyone else was in here. *Crush-a-snowflake!* If anyone saw my shoes, they would know. I watched most of the girls on the dance floor, and mine, I'd have to say, stood out.

I heard the lid from a lipstick snap. Then a slow tap-tap from the pair of heels moved deeper into the room. The girl opened the stall next to mine.

A metal click followed a puff of air, then a dreaded tap-tap against my stall wall.

I wanted to say, "Nevermore," but felt the joke would be wasted on the clueless.

There was another quick wrapping against the stall.

I didn't want to talk, but then I thought maybe they needed paper and I wouldn't want to drip dry either.

"Yeah?" My question echoed.

The girl's voice held remorse, "Juslynn?"

I clamped my hands over my mouth. It was Cher.

"I know you can hear me."

What did I do to deserve this? Heaving a lengthy sigh … I didn't bother to answer myself, realizing I didn't care anymore.

"This is between you and me, but I wanted to say, 'Thanks.'"

Completely caught off guard, I thought she read my thoughts. "What?"

"Thanks for not getting me in trouble at work. I need the job so I can get away from here, you know, away from them."

She was talking about her family and sharing her troubles with me. This side of her creeped me out, a little. I leaned against the tiled wall and dropped my guard. "What do you want from me, Cher?"

"Listen… just listen, and don't interrupt, this is important."

"Uh-huh."

"I mean it."

"Okay," I snapped.

"Juslynn, I would be the first to say, I don't believe our futures are written in Fate's concrete slab of destiny. And if I could in any way, convince you not to overreact tonight, will you try not too?"

"What's that supposed to mean?"

"Please, please don't tell anyone what I'm about to do or say," Cher begged.

Concerned for my well-being, I flew out of the stall, and almost smacked right into her. "What are you talking about?"

Cher grabbed my hands and stared into my eyes. No, more like past me, as if I wasn't there. Needless to say, it freaked me out.

The voice coming out of her was distant like she was on the other end of a bad cell connection. "You've set your path in motion. You must release your desires. You cannot force fate. You must deviate from the path of regret. For tonight, may be too late, for the both of you to mess with fate."

I yanked away from her hard and hissed, "You're crazy."

With panic swirling in her eyes, she whispered, "I know." Swiveling away from me, she checked the mirror and then smoothed out her dress. "Honestly, I just thought one good turn deserves another.

"Most of the time, I try to ignore the voices, but when they are this strong, I tend to listen. This one wouldn't leave me alone, and it almost sounded familiar. Definitely parental, like a female conscience. Which is why I wanted it to go away. I don't need another mother hanging around me."

Pointing a manicured nail at me, Cher ended her rant with, "Oh, and don't ask me about the message; I have no idea what it means. That's for you to figure out."

She turned on the tip of her shoe and left without another word.

My night just turned into an episode of Supernatural; someone cue Sam and Dean.

CHAPTER THIRTEEN

A hand clasped my upper arm, and I squeaked, causing me to step back into my rotten reality.

"Hey girl, where have you been? Wade is getting tired, and my feet are cramping." Fern was rocking from side to side, to confirm she was in pain.

"We just got here twenty minutes ago. You want to leave now?"

Fern wrinkled her nose and sniffed toward my face. "Are you buzzed? We've been here for over two hours. Have you seen Britney and Keith? I think they went back to the limo, but then again, if the driver is there…" Her voice trailed off.

"Wait? Two hours?" I dug into my clutch for my cell phone. Swiping the screen 8:43 p.m. lit across Spaz's snout. Then I notice three missed calls from my dad and two text messages from Carter.

Not wanting to read Carter's text, possibly telling me he went home. I pressed to listen to my messages. Dad's first message seemed normal.

"Hey, J-baby, how's the dance going? Was wondering if

you needed a ride home? Call me or Karia back soon, so we don't make any plans to catch a movie." Karia mumbled, and then there was laughing between the two of them. He chortled before saying, "Okay or other plans. Anyway, call me back."

Eww, if they didn't stop acting like newlyweds I was going to be scarred for life.

Then his voice crackled through the receiver as the second message played. "Juslynn, it's Dad. Can you call me? Something's come up, and I need to talk to you. Maybe if you could come home early? I know, that's not what you want to hear, but we need to talk. Call me."

My face fell, and Fern tapped my hand. "What's up?" She kept rocking back and forth.

"Hold on." I pressed my hand against my open ear so I could hear.

Dave's casual tone had changed to a mix of panic and terseness. "Juslynn. I mean it, damn it!" There was a faint layering of white static over his words. I could only make out a few words, but then I focused on my dad's threat. "Call me back, or I'm coming to yank you out of there." His breathing seemed hard and short as though he sprinted five hundred yards. "Forget it. I'm not waiting. I'm coming." There was more gargled static then… nothing.

"She will never fly," was nothing more than a fabrication my mind had selectively picked from out of the noise. *Or was it?* A chill traced its fingers down my back causing temporary paralysis.

Laughter, music, and holiday chatter filled the hallway in a jumbled overlay of clatter. There was a faint touch on my cheek that brought me back.

Fern had stopped moving. "Juslynn?"

Shuddering, I whispered, "Something's wrong. My dad is on his way here."

"Are you in trouble?"

"I don't think so. The way he spoke, it wasn't normal."

"Maybe something happened to Karia?" The question was used to help calm me, but I thought if that were the case he would have said so.

"I need to find Carter and tell him I have to go."

Fern's features hardened. "I haven't seen him since he danced with Cher." She wouldn't look at me. "I was looking for you because I thought you two had a fight. Then I started to think both of you left." Rolling her eyes at the ceiling, she continued. "You have to admit; he was acting pretty strange. I mean, we're all friends but, well, I don't know."

"Just say it. My night can't get any worse."

"He seemed torn on how to act. I watched the way he looked at you Juslynn. I believe your best friend likes you more than friends, but he is holding back for some reason." She blew out hard. "Carter seems conflicted."

"Fern, you watch too many movies. This is reality and," I considered the caged gym clock, "my reality is about to change for the worse when my dad gets here."

Fern's eyes bugged. "What if your dad thinks the same about Carter? Would that change the dynamic on how he feels about your friendship with him? Maybe he's worried you might do something, you know, physical."

Then I remembered our botched father-daughter talk last night and how he insinuated he couldn't handle my female issues. Peeved, I allowed the emotion to eat away at my uneasiness.

I slipped my phone back in the clutch. "Hey, can you do me a favor?"

"Sure."

"If you see Carter, tell him I left; and to give me a few days before calling me. Can you also tell the others, I'm sorry for bailing? I'll call you and Brie tomorrow, okay?"

"Are you sure you're going to be all right?"

"Sure. I always bounce back."

We said goodnight and parted. Fern left to find the others while I cut through the crowd to get to the check-in booth for my cape.

A girl I knew from Calculus was dipped in front of me by her partner. So much was on my mind I couldn't remember her name. She pointed at me and smiled. "Hey, great party."

"Yeah, well have fun; I'm on my way out." I tried to cut to the side of her.

She stopped in front of me, and in a perky voice, said, "Hey, I think I saw your date head out that way," and then gestured in the direction where we came in.

"Oh, okay, thanks. I was wondering where he went off to."

"'Merry Christmas or Happy Holidays,' I never know what to say."

"Last Christmas I Gave You My Heart" blared through the speakers.

"Yes, Merry Christmas," I yelled over the song's lyrics. This particular tune I hated. Then I wished the equipment would short out. As I approached the ticket booth, the gym's lights dimmed. A crack amplified through the speakers creating a high-pitched whine, then silence.

Ambling toward the table, I dug for the ticket I needed to retrieve my cape.

A different girl was working this shift. She flipped a mound of curls back to push her hands against her ears. "Oww."

I gave her a weak smile of agreement. "Here." I waved the little piece of paper at her. "It's a white, floor-length cape."

She took it and checked the number. "Sure thing, I'll be right back."

The vice-principle picked up a mic and tapped it. "Sorry, ladies and gents. There is a slight mishap with a fuse. Please be patient. Someone is checking on it. Give us five minutes before we play the last song."

I opened my purse and checked the time on my cell's screen. It was 8:55 p.m. and positive, my dad, was outside fuming over who-knows-what.

The girl returned, interrupting my thought. "I'm surprised how light it is." Before releasing my cape, the girl gave it one last pat. "It's lovely."

I placed my clutch on the table to take it from her. Then draped it over my shoulders before fastening the clasp. Since I was heading out, I raised the hood over my flat curls. *I mean what did it matter? Who was I going to impress, now that Carter was MIA?*

Thanking the girl, I turned to walk out the doors. Another crackled hiss came through the speakers. The noise almost made me jump out of my skin as I placed a hand on the handle. Heat licked each finger like something was warning me not to go.

The DJ began to apologize for the equipment malfunction and ended his explanation with a few school announcements about winter break. He added a few Ho-Ho-Ho's before stating, "Hope you all get what you wanted from 'The Man.'"

Depressed, I opened the door. All I wanted was to be kissed for the first time, by Carter. One real, raise-your-foot, soar in the clouds, kiss.

The breeze hit me with swirling snow. There was a funny ache in the middle of my chest, radiating to the back of my shoulder blades.

When I thought of Carter, I was getting used to the

heartache, but this was different. Dread stirred me enough to check my surroundings. Two voices, one whispering, the other deep and menacing, echoed from down the hall.

Unable to stop my feet from moving, I headed to find the source.

Turning a corner, I saw them. Carter and Cher. She was pressed against the brick wall and Carter was leaning toward her, talking in a very hushed tone. It appeared he had an ominous red glow outlining his features. But since I was in shock, it could have been the hall's emergency lights playing tricks on me.

Cher turned in my direction. A smile dipping in wicked delight played across her lips. In the middle of a blink, she pushed her face against Carter's, and kissed him.

The heartbreak that came from within shook me down to my soul. When the echo from my pained wail reverberated, he jumped away from her.

Staggering back, Carter whipped around to yell at Cher. Then he ran straight for me.

All my senses shut down.

Nothing seemed real anymore. Not my family. Not my friends. Neither Carter's friendship nor the feelings I carried for him. Even my nemesis was in on the act, pretending to care. Cher feeding me some hocus-pocus warning to get me to trust her enough to leave so she could have Carter all to herself.

Carter shouted, "Hold on."

His command broke the spell I was under. Abruptly, I pushed off of my toes and ran. Where I was running to, I didn't care.

Reaching the outside corridor, I kept pressing on. The wind caught my cape, pulling it behind me. It furled and floated causing me to overcompensate for my balance.

I felt like White Riding Hood running away from the wolf.

Through blurred vision, I saw my dad. He called out to me, waving his hands.

Carter's voice boomed from behind. "Juslynn, stop!"

I ran for the stairs, toward my dad.

The limo driver yelled from the parking lot, "You cannot deny her fate. It is her time."

Stealing one last glance at the man who ripped my heart out; I flew down the iced-over stairs. Running on my toes to gain more speed, I grabbed the railing for balance. My right foot hit the last stair wrong. The heel slipped to the side. A sickening crunch followed, but my momentum continued causing both legs to slide out from under me.

My dad and Carter both shouted, *"No!"*

In a split-second, I knew this was going to end badly for me, and the crunch I heard was the back of my skull striking the bottom concrete step.

CHAPTER FOURTEEN

I tried to breathe. But my mouth wouldn't open, and the sense of claustrophobia grew. When I moved my hand; it felt lighter than usual. There was a faint rustle of plastic as I squirmed.

My eyelids fluttered open and was greeted by complete darkness.

I gasped, but couldn't feel the air pass my lips. My five senses were on the fritz. It wasn't hot or cold. I couldn't see or smell. The only sensation I felt was similar to floating in a pool.

Flustered, I tried to use my voice.

Nothing.

Collecting all of my strength, I tried again.

Nothing.

Using my fingers to feel around, both hands plunged into something above me.

"Hey!" A raspy voice whispered.

Trickles of panic filled my throat. Someone was in here

with me. I focused on talking; using thought to picture my tongue, throat, moving both lips to form the words.

"Hel... lo..." It felt shaky.

Emptiness responded.

Then I started to wonder how I ended here in the first place. *Wasn't I at the dance? Where were my friends? My dad? ...Carter?*

The sensation of falling made my stomach flip-flop. I must have passed out and was in the hospital. Maybe it was the middle of the night. It would explain why I felt so disoriented.

A slow hiss came from above. "You're new."

Was the patient above me?

Then a male uttered from my left. "What happened to you?"

Panicked, I tried to speak again but couldn't. To calm myself I counted backward. An image of cotton balls being stuffed into my mouth came into mind, and each round piece of fluff was another question. If I could get the cotton out of my mouth, *what question would be most important?*

A meek string of words rose from below. "Give this body some time. She just got here."

Time?

"It takes a while to form thought to speech." The small voice said.

Thought to voice?

A gruff inquiry floated down, "I wonder what happens from here?"

Using the picture method again, made me project the thought that I was nursing a sore throat. "Where am I?"

"It speaks." One of them said.

"Stop it," echoed from below. "This one only has a few hours before dormancy sets in again."

"Mine was by fire." A raspy reply wheezed.

The response from my right said, "Car accident."

A deep tenor on my left asked, "What happened to you?"

"Happened?" …was all I could manage.

An innocent child-like question drifted from below me, "Yes, how did you die?"

Beyond terrified, several memories flashed through my mind's eye. Wet, ice-coated stairs, my dad by the car and Carter's face when I glanced back, there was a blur, a starless night sky. Each one flipped faster than the last, images before my death.

The scream that broke free from me was loud enough to wake the living.

The next night*

Once again, I was met by darkness and slithering sentences. Each voice added more information as to what was happening. Why I lost time and only remembered certain things. The reasons they believed we were cursed. A few more had joined in the discussion by the time I could understand their sentences. It still freaked me out trying to comprehend where I was.

Unfortunately, seeing darkness colored my depression deep-space black. Maybe, this is what it felt like to be in a black hole. Here but not—emotions so heavy my subconscious might implode.

Night three… I think*

. . .

A metal door opened and then latched closed. The bodies filling the drawers in the morgue were quiet. Most had passed their roaming times. It left me alone to dwell on being dead.

I wondered if this was what my mom went through. Thoughts of worry swamped me about my dad and how he would cope with another loss. *Would his new wife be able to handle if he disappeared emotionally?* I longed to have the ability to check on him, talk to him one more time. Find out why he was so upset and the unexpected urgency to speak with me.

When this string of burdens burned out, I would light a new one. Thinking of my friends, my dog, the future I would never have, and the kiss I would never experience.

Yes, I found it fascinating, the anger and desire I felt when I was alive came with me. I wondered if Carter cared I was gone, or possibly relieved. Despite fighting my thoughts, his smile would still break through. Memory would reproduce his laugh. How I wanted to run my fingers through his messy locks. But the one feature I tried desperately to burn away was his eyes.

My subconscious would paint them blue, and I would force them to change to brown or even hazel. I didn't care for the color hazel; it was such an odd mishmash for an iris.

The double ring from a phone vibrated the airwaves.

One of the morticians must be back from break. I never could see the male clearly, but I recognized his speech pattern. I was starting to fade. Using my ability, I envisioned a ribbon and tied it around me. Then I focused on staying tethered.

Classic piano played again. He answered it on the third downbeat. I aimed my focus to the middle of the room. There was a flash of dim light. It was similar to peering through an ice cube; I tracked the distance his words had to travel to the other side of the gurney tables.

The man kept pacing. I listened harder. Then the room tilted like I had done the action myself to hear him better.

"So, they will be in tomorrow to claim the girl? Sure, I'll have the release paperwork ready. The autopsy report is in your in-basket, it needs your signature."

There was a long pause.

He scratched his head. "Yeah, I know the Vaxtons. It's a shame about Dave having to bury his daughter too. Don't worry; I took excellent notes. The cause of death was pretty straightforward."

Another pause, I didn't know how much time I had left, but he was talking about me, and I didn't want to miss anything significant.

"It's a tragedy she died from a slip and fall."

Yes, I agreed. It was a tragedy because I couldn't say I died from a fire saving kittens, fell from a cliff rock climbing, or by an icicle falling on me; no, I died by failed footwear.

CHAPTER FIFTEEN

I awoke to humming.

This time the environment was different. A desperate need to escape from my confinement made me twitch nervously. My fingertips brushed against soft material. Both eyes snapped open. At first, the darkness was disorientating, but after a few blinks I could make out white fabric draped in a diamond pattern with big white buttons securing the material above my face.

What is this?

My senses were coming back online. I could see and touch without concentrating on using thought. A suffocating mix of chilled earth and stale air made me choke and gag. Anxiously, my body wanted to stand. Answering my desire, was an unusual pressure that wrapped around my waist. I had no choice but to obey as it yanked me from my position.

Momentarily, I felt alive again, even as the wind cleansed the stale taste of dirt from my nose and mouth. Dazed, I focused on the dimly lit sky until little points of light burned through. I sighed the word, "Stars."

Sluggishly, I scanned the area. Big trees, in a sporadic pattern, became clearer. A little lower, the ground came into view. Different sized rocks were all around me. Then I blinked again. No, not rocks, but tombstones. Confused, I scrunched up my face. "A cemetery?"

Everything wore a fresh blanket of snow as though the area purposely dressed up for my arrival. I was starting to feel overwhelmed as my senses sharpened beyond a twenty/twenty eyesight. I could see the cracks in the headstones and old statues, the intricate groove patterns in the tree bark, to each crystallized pine needle that glistened in the moonlight. Absorbing all of this magnified the fact I was alone. Both arms unconsciously wrapped around my middle to help contain the growing sadness.

That is until I heard humming again.

Its sorrowful melody was so alluring that I dared to seek out the source. The snow never crunched under my footfalls. It felt as though I was walking above it. Another step and I noticed my foot didn't sink, there was no impression. I held out my hands and watched in amazement and horror, every single ice flake float right through them.

I forgot about the humming.

"You know, you'll get used to it. We all do over time."

The male talking meant nothing as I stood there witnessing the impossible. A sob bubbled from somewhere inside as reality slapped my face. As I peered through my hands, I noticed mounds of frozen funeral bouquets, stuffed animals, and used candles coated in fresh snow. In this exact moment, all my doubts and denial evaporated...

I was dead.

When I fell to my knees, I noticed I was still wearing my prom dress, cape, and shoes. Damn these stupid shoes. I tried to take them off, but my hands passed right through. Frustration grew as I furiously worked to remove the heels. My vision blurred indicating I was about to shed tears.

"You know, you're only wasting your energy." His smugness lit a keg of irritation within me.

I used the emotion's power to help me speak, "What do you know? Why do you even care?"

"Well, I can't say; but it's hard for new spirits to accept what is final. Like I said, 'we were all there once.'" His words faded, and then I heard the snow crunch under something heavy. Alarmed, I scooted back and gazed at where my right hand landed. It was my mother's headstone.

Timidly I used a finger to trace her name in the smoky, marble setting. Cerena Faye Vaxton, Loving wife, and mother. My dad had personalized it with 'You gave me wings, now you have yours.' While I read the inscription to myself, there was a glint of reflected moonlight, to the right of me.

A plastic marker was spiked into the ground a few feet away. Since I couldn't pick it up, I leaned over and read, "Plot 1218, Vaxton, Juslynn Ann. Born: 01-09-1999 Died: 12-18-2016. The light in our world has lost its luster, but heaven is now a brighter place."

I placed both hands on either side of the card and attempted to cry.

With a heavy sigh, he simply stated, "I can see I have my work cut out for me."

What did that mean? All I wanted was my life back. To see my dad and Karia, again. To drink coffee with my friends at the Buzz. To hold and walk my dog. To swallow my fear and tell Carter how I really felt about him. If I had, then maybe, I would still be breathing.

Hunched over and going through the motions of crying, I didn't notice his presence. A pair of black boots stopped in front of me. They were solid.

Following my gaze skyward, I beheld a man, close to my age. His smile was cool and bright as the snow. Deep blue, tinted lips parted as his smile widen enough to make me wary. Following his features to his eyes; my breath would have been sucked from my lungs if there was air to give. Two, black light, purple orbs stared down at me.

The ultraviolet glow radiating from them was mesmerizing. His hair hung in inky black locks, with a hint of midnight blue from where the moonlight dared to touch. A pale, long-fingered hand reached for me.

Without even thinking, my right hand slipped into his.

The smile he wore turned upside down as he released me as fast as he pulled me upright.

He spoke while shaking his hand as if he was in pain. "It seems this will complicate things between us, Little Layer."

"Where am I? What will? Why did you call me that? Who are you?"

He hummed for a bit, while circling me, and then answered. "Our kind don't normally mesh well together."

"Huh?"

In a grand flourish, he extended his arms out. "Welcome to the afterlife, Nephilim." Then he answered each of my questions in rapid secession. "Unfortunately, you were more in touch with your human side. I called you a Layer because only half of your soul has crossed over; this half is hanging on to wants you can't have. And you'll find out who I am in due time."

I held a hand up and squinted. "I'm a what?"

"Nephilim."

"No, I'm not."

"Look, I've been around for a long time, and I know a Nephilim when I see, or in this case, touch one. So, you can drop the act."

"I'm dead," I shouted. It felt good to hear my voice at full volume.

The guy bent his knees to balance himself on the back of his boots. "Yes... you... are..." Then his eyes captured my attention as I watched the purple glow dim while he studied me. "But I see we have a bigger problem. You don't know what you are. Which also means you haven't even begun your training." He rocked back, placing one arm under his chest to position the other so he could tap his face in thought. "I can't believe, she would leave you this helpless."

"Look, creeper. My name is Juslynn Va..." I couldn't remember my last name all of a sudden. "Juslynn Vax..." I glanced down at the plastic marker. "Vaxton. I was born here in Bothell." The state, I wasn't sure. "I've lived here with my family and friends. I have... a... dog." Its name I couldn't recall. "I'm graduating high school this year. And no one has ever said, 'Hey Juslynn we need to talk, oh and by the way you're... an... angel.'"

The last three words tasted bitter as visions from the night of the dance tugged on my memories. I remembered my dad had left a few messages, but it was the last one that left an impression. He was angry. No, more like on edge.

The male interrupted my thoughts. "Nephilim," he said with a teacher's tone.

"Stop calling me that."

"You are only half angel; a Nephilim. We wouldn't be having this conversation if you were a full angel."

"Okay, smart guy. If I'm part angel and human why did you call me a Layer?"

"You've packed extra baggage for this trip, and it has you bound here. You'll have to unpack or chuck it before you can move on. It will only complicate matters, and you can't become an actual angel until the human bond is severed. And, well, demons don't typically help angels unless we can strike a deal.

"Oh, and by the way, you can call me Haste. I've been assigned to you as your Keeper, or your worst nightmare. Both descriptions are correct, so what you decide to call me; I'll leave that up to you."

CHAPTER SIXTEEN

Stunned, I stood in the snow. Even in death, someone was going to tell me what to do. Well, before he started bossing me around I needed answers.

"Why do I roam?"

"Your spirit is stuck in limbo until the tainted emotions you carry are resolved. It's your choice to, A.) Let go of your emotional anchor and become what you are meant to be." He shuddered. "B.) The ones you left behind could also have you chained here. Their inability to let you go will keep you in this state. Or there is always C.), both parties refuse to let go and you remain tethered between life and death. Which means you won't be able to fulfill your duties to become a full-fledged angel and I remain your Keeper as you slowly become… more like me." His grin turned into a dark chuckle.

I bristled. "Okay, how did I become a Nephilim? Can I undo the spell, curse, or do a chant so I can get my life back?"

"Really? I can't believe they've kept you in the dark for so long." The surprise in his statement was backhanded. Haste spun and marched over to a traditional headstone to lean against it. "No wonder you've been having such a hard time on this side. You remind me of a helpless baby bird some rotten kid knocked from its nest." His snicker had a hissing undertone, which reminded me of what he was.

"I'm glad you find this humorous."

"I do in fact. Your pain is exquisite, very tasty. Maybe, we'll forego the lesson, and I'll just keep you for my own."

I whipped the cape's hood off my head. "You'll what?"

"Keep you, Little Layer. You know nothing about who you are or what you can do. What good is a half-breed angel who doesn't know what she can turn into?" Haste grimaced.

I sauntered over to him remembering he didn't like touching me. Using one finger, I poked him in the chest.

He flinched. "Hey!" Then rubbed the area as both eyes narrowed.

I, on the other hand, felt nothing. There was a positive side to being dead after all. Unable to hide my pleasure, from getting a little of my own back, I smirked. "How do I know if what you are saying is the truth? You may be my Keeper, but you said so yourself, you are a demon. Religions, myths, and lore state demons can't be trusted, why should I trust you?"

Haste continued to brush at the spot where I'd poked him. Adjusting his crisp, black button-down shirt, he eyed me. "Someone's gotten bold."

"Why don't you explain our roles?"

The demon began to pace almost stepping on my mother's headstone.

My hands flew up. "Haste."

The big leather boot hung in midair before he took a step up and continued to pace two-feet above the ground. My mouth hung open watching this six-foot being defy gravity. Haste did an about-face and marched over to me. He smacked under my chin to close my mouth.

"Ouch!" *Totally felt that.* I rubbed my chin. "How?"

"You think your touch is the only one that can inflict pain? Any kind of power current can work both ways." He pointed to the ground. "You are grounded, I'm not. Get it? Also, keep in mind, I am your Keeper, and as such we have a bond. Who do you think helped you out of your grave?"

I rubbed my middle remembering the sensation. "Look, how do I go back, move on, fulfill my duties? I'm not sure I want to be bound to you."

"What makes you think you have a say?" His question didn't have the tone of a rhetorical, but almost challenging.

"Haste, tell me what I need to do? I feel out of place here. As my Keeper what are your duties?"

"My role is not what you think. I can give you the tools on, how to pass on but I am your keeper in that way. If you remain here you turn into a demon, like me. I 'keep,'" he used two fingers on each hand to empathize keep, "you here."

I took several steps back. "You're going to turn me into a demon?"

His face hardened, but there was a tinge of sadness around both eyes. "You make it sound as though it's a bad thing." My hand rose to his exposed stomach, and he shifted. To protect himself, he looped both arms in front of him and glared.

I shrieked, "I don't want to be a demon." Both arms jutted out while waving my hands to keep him from invading my space.

"You're jumping the gun. I'm supposed to offer you a choice. Then you answer." He was testy, and his eyes shifted to an orange hue.

The change of color made me rethink my actions. I must have offended him. And before I could stop myself, I blurted, "I'm sorry."

His face turned to stone. Both eyes dulled to a cool violet. "You're what?"

"I'm sorry. Please continue." Self-preservation had me on high alert as I clutched my cloak closer to me.

His demeanor was posturing, but there was softness around his mouth. "No one has ever apologized to me in this form. Why did you say that?"

I half shrugged. "I interrupted you, and even though, I'm upset, you're not the cause of my demise. Besides, it was wrong of me to judge. You are trying to help me," I thought about what I just said and finished with, "well, sort of. But, I am sorry."

"And you meant it, didn't you?"

"Yes." *Where was he going with this?*

"Nephilim, either you are extremely lucky or extremely smart. From your show of respect to a demon, I will guide you. But as your Keeper, I can't say I won't try to trip you up along the way. I still have my duties to fulfill."

"You'll help me?"

"Yes, if that's what you want."

"Okay, what do I do?"

"Do you want to be bound as a demon or walk among the stars?" He cast his gaze upward.

"I want to unpack my baggage. I wasn't going to get what I wanted anyway." My body was becoming more transparent.

Haste arched an eyebrow. "Let the battle of wits commence. We will start tomorrow night."

CHAPTER SEVENTEEN

This night held more meaning for me. I was anxious as my roaming time began. Coughing the dust from my lungs, Haste pulled me from the grave.

He was laughing.

"Still find my situation funny, I see."

"No, what I find funny, is you. Okay, first and foremost, you are dead. Stop acting alive. You do not need to breathe, eat, or cry. You're not attached to your body anymore. Just because your spirit wakes up in the box doesn't mean you are really in the box. Understand?"

I picked pretend debris from my cape so I wouldn't have to look at him. "No."

"No? Never mind, you'll catch on."

"Why do I awake at night? Why not when the sun comes up or at dusk when the sun goes down?"

"Time has a sense of humor. You arise the second after you died. Your life ended at 9:02 p.m. You'll wake up at 9:02 and whatever second was after your last breath. Your roaming state is the same for all spirits, you have six hours."

"Why only six?"

"I'm not exactly sure. It just is. So, with that being said, we better get started. You've already used up several days, and you are on your second hour for tonight."

I looked at him shocked. "I awoke over an hour ago?"

"Yup. Now pay attention. We have a lot to cover if you want to cross over in time." He brushed his bangs back.

"There is a time frame? Why didn't you say so last night?"

"Um, hello? Keeper. Be thankful; I'm helping you now."

"I am. Thank you."

Shooting me a half cocky grin, he said, "Look, being nice isn't always going to get you your way."

Ignoring him, I asked, "What do I need to do?"

"You need to unload your human emotions, and to do so, you need to do the opposite of what you felt when you died."

"You make it seem so simple." I rolled my eyes.

"Because it is, unless you don't want to try, and would rather stay with me?" Haste winked. "We could be wicked together."

I found myself feeling flattered, a little. "Thanks, Haste, but you said our kind doesn't mesh well. Your words, not mine."

His smile became mischievous. "True, but if you became a demon…"

"Time isn't on my side, and you're playing me. What do I need to do?"

He cleared his throat. "Okay, you are going to learn the basics of haunting. You need to find out who is anchoring you here and at the same time release your emotions. Wipe your slate clean."

"Okay, what do I do first?"

"Ask for passage from your Keeper."

"Passage to where? I don't know who would want to keep me here."

Haste walked past me toward my grave marker and stood there, arms crossed, glaring at me. "Really? You can't think of anyone?"

Exasperated, I tossed my arms in the air. "Why don't you tell me?"

"Keeper."

"Thanks a lot. So, I'm supposed to ask for you to take me to the person keeping me here, but you can't tell me who?"

"No, I can but where is the sport in that? Besides, if you follow my crumbs you might find your way."

"Crumbs? So, this really is a game to you?"

He shrugged.

I marched on air over to him. "Who is keeping me here?"

His gaze dropped from mine.

I looked down at my mother's grave and reread the passage.

"Haste, please take me to my dad."

In a blink, we were gone.

CHAPTER EIGHTEEN

Friday, December 23rd, 2016.

We materialized in my kitchen. I could feel the tears but knew they weren't real, remembering what Haste said. There was a smell in the air, burnt coffee maybe. The room was dark, but I could make out a figure in the chair by the back door.

Dave was hunched over. I thought he was sleeping. Walking over, my heels made no sound as I approached him. Then I noticed a pill bottle in front of him.

I snapped at Haste. "Is this a joke? Are you playing me?"

"No joke. The truth, in this case, is much more palatable. He has imploded emotionally. The hole is growing and will soon consume him."

"What am I supposed to do?" I asked in a panic.

"He needs to release you like he finally did with your mother."

"How do you know about her? And that took my dad almost three years to get over her."

"So?"

"You said I'm on a short timeline. I don't have years. Heck, I don't even have weeks."

Haste looked at the ceiling. "Careful, angel, don't swear."

"Give me a clue. An extra roll of the dice. A get-out-of-jail-free card." I pleaded.

"Hello? Demon. I've been around. Honestly, maybe you are lucky, and you'll find the answer..." He blew on his nails and pretended to polish them against his shirt. Then huffed, "Or not."

I tried to crouch down next to my dad. I glanced at the brown bottle, clearly noting it was still full. But the stare he wore gave me concern. I stood to talk to Haste when a light flickered on in the hallway.

My dad quickly grabbed the bottle and hid it under his arm.

Karia stopped right before the kitchen archway. "Dave, please come to bed."

He sighed. "I will in a minute."

"Please let me in. We can grieve together. I miss her too."

"Karia, go to bed. I'll be there in a minute."

"But?"

He slammed his fist down on the table. "If I only had gotten to her in time? Explained to her what was really going on."

"Dave, I don't understand. Was she in danger? Why did you go to the dance that night?" She inched her way into the kitchen.

There was a ring of warmth rolling off of her. I focused on the feeling and found myself floating through the center island toward my step-mother. When I was close enough, I saw a pinpoint of light coming from her belly.

Oh my gosh. Karia was pregnant, and my dad was going to do something devastating. I needed to stop him.

My Keeper coughed behind me. I peered back, and he motioned for me to act.

I pointed at him. "Can they hear you?"

"No."

Then I pointed at me. "Can they hear me?"

"Maybe?"

I placed a hand on my hip. "You're not going to tell me?"

He started humming again. I assumed that was my answer.

"Thanks a lot," I clipped.

With both hands extended, I reached out, careful to not press my hands through her stomach. Thinking about it grossed me out. But, I kept my palms against her belly. There was a faint heartbeat. I felt giddy, then sad when I realized I wouldn't be here to help out with my sister or brother.

She cleared her throat. "Dave, please come to bed soon. I'm not feeling well, and I need to lie down."

A small whine stole my attention. Spaz was staring at me. I bent down until we were eye to eye. "Hey boy. You being good?" I reached out to pet him, and he backed up growling.

Dave didn't even turn around. "Karia, take the dog with you."

Coming across as tired, she said, "Come on Spaz, let's go to bed." Karia turned slowly, and I watched her click the light switch off.

My dad looked at the bottle again then placed it on the table.

Was he really thinking about taking his life because of me? I floated back over to him. Even if he couldn't hear me, I had to try.

"Dad?"

He dropped his gaze at the bottle.

"Dad," I shrieked.

Haste snickered.

Both men peeved me to the point I needed to react physically. I wanted to hit the both of them so bad my fingers tingled. The sensation began to blossom and pool in the palm of my hand.

My dad reached for the bottle.

I smacked it so hard it went sailing through the air and hit the window by the back door. The window cracked. The room was quiet except for the plastic bottle spinning on the floor.

Dave jumped from his chair.

Haste stopped laughing.

I stared at my hand.

The moment broke when my dad whispered, "Juslynn?"

Both men were staring into the darkness around me. Haste was in thought. Dave blindly scanned the room. I remained stationary, trying to calculate my next move.

My hand gave me an idea. He needed a reason to let go of me but at the same time a reason to keep living. I knew he loved Karia, but if there was a way I could reveal to him what I found out, it might knock some sense into him.

Wrapping myself in sorrow and disappointment, I approached my father. I looked at my hand again, and whispered, "This has to work."

Quickly, I glanced at Haste to see if he caught on to what I was going to attempt. He held his position with no emotion on his face. The only inkling of existence was the faint purple glowing from his eyes. Haste appeared more demon at this moment, and it frightened me some, but I continued with my plan.

My dad needed to know.

I rushed him, circle once, and placed my hand over his eyes. It was strange to see his face through my hand. Shaking away the creepiness of it, I tried to recreate the warmth I felt from a small spark of life. Then I hit him with my emotional cocktail. And for extra measure, I released what I felt for my mother when she died.

Dave's eyes glistened. He was hoarse from being dowsed with so many emotions. "I didn't know." His anguish mixed with mine. "I love you. I failed you and your mother. I couldn't protect her either. She made me promise not to tell you what happened the day she died."

I forced my hand to stay still. Using my abilities, I turned my words into thought. "What Dad? What couldn't you tell me?"

Tears dripped from his chin and nose. "Your mother was a half-breed. You have angel blood flowing through..." His sentence trailed away, and then he regained his composure. "Had flowing through your veins."

Trembling, I gazed at my Keeper. His smirk said, *"See, I told you."*

I pressed more images into Dave's mind. Our time spent as a family, father-daughter moments, the day I picked out Spaz, and the last Christmas before Mom passed away.

"The good time's dad. You need them to help build the future." Then I hit him with Karia and the life she was carry-ing. "I won't be here to help, and she needs you now, more than ever."

I took a shallow breath and Haste grumbled under his.

"Dad, the future is waiting for you. I'm the past, and with my new role, you must let me go."

Startled, he faced me. Looking through my hand at the cracked window, Dave sighed, and then started sobbing. He reached out where I was standing.

I didn't understand until I saw my reflection in the pane of glass. He could see me. My outline thinned like vapor. I was fading.

"Dad, they need you. I need you to be there for them. I don't want to leave, but I have to go." I wanted to cry. "Please live, and enjoy your life. I love you, Dad."

He watched the window then bent down to kiss me on the head. I barely felt the press of his lips. "I trapped your mom for three years. I won't trap you too. Go, find your wings, princess. I love you Juslynn, and I release you."

A shimmer of light brightened my outline causing a burning in the middle of my back. "Ouch." I turned to Haste. "You didn't tell me releasing would hurt."

"One down," Haste said while pretending he was looking at a watch. "Wherever you drift off to, you better be thinking about whom else needs to release you. You only have two days left before you are trapped here, or you can always ask to be..."

"Wait. How much time does a Layer have before they're trapped here?"

"You have seven days. That means if you can't achieve both A and B, in the requirements of crossing, I get a present for Christmas."

I lunged at him, but my hands turned to mist before I could wrap them around his neck.

CHAPTER NINETEEN

Saturday, December 24th, 2016, Christmas Eve.

If Haste was right, it was December twenty-fourth. And there were only two nights left for me to find who was holding me here. I was dragging my feet about releasing my desires for Carter. Thinking about him made my silent heart, ache.

A few days ago, I would have given almost anything to feel him sigh in my arms. I was slipping into unfamiliar territory, for my desire for him was changing. I missed talking to him. Sitting at the same table in the library and reading comics when we were supposed to be studying. His friendship meant the world to me.

Haste said with attitude, "What his friendship means, is incorrect, or did you forget?"

My thoughts jammed. "Haste? Did you read my mind?"

"Read, no; listen, yes."

I felt violated and created some distance between us.

Standing over the frozen bouquets, I knelt down to stare at the white lilies. They were Fern's favorite. I couldn't grasp the one I was looking at. As I tried to poke it, a small square of paper slipped out.

It was a picture of Britney, Fern and me at last year's car wash fundraiser. A knot formed where I tried to swallow. I missed them terribly.

Smiling, I whispered, "Thanks, girls, for the reminder."

"Haste, my time waster, take me to my friends."

"Yeah. I may be able to listen to your thoughts, but I'm not a mind reader. That's an entirely different kind of demon." He wiped the snow from my plot marker. That was very non-demon like. "You need to give me a specific name and image of the human you want to connect with."

Haste chuckled as he lifted a stuffed cat with devil horns.

Snickering, I said, "I see the similarity." Then I recalled Fern won it last year from one of those claw machines. *Was Haste dropping a crumb?*

I reached out and placed my hand on his shoulder. "Haste, please take me to Fern."

Before we faded, he winked at me.

The darkness in Fern's bedroom held an ominous weight to it. It sucked the air from the space and made me shudder. The moonlight couldn't pass through the closed drapes.

There was a sniff and hiccup from the corner by the night-stand. I walked through her bed to see both of my friends huddled into the corner. Fern held a rectangular piece of paper. It was the card I had left behind. The grip she had on Carter's card was turning her knuckles white.

Brie held Fern's shoulders and sobbed.

It seemed as though, both of them were hanging on to me. Positioning myself in front of them I squatted, and then tried to move Fern's red locks from her face with my fingers. Honestly, it made me feel special they were missing me this much.

"That's my girl. They have each other. Let's leave them to work out their misery." My Keeper knelt next to me and looped an arm around mine. His touch made me wince.

"No." I broke away from him. Lifting both hands, I placed them over their eyes. Flipping through my mind, I remembered the car wash and how much fun it was. I pictured us on her bathroom floor and Brie telling us she was getting married.

A ping of misery stabbed me in the chest, realizing I wouldn't be attending. No, this needed to be done. We all needed to let go.

Brie lifted her head and wiped both eyes.

I was glad she couldn't see me, the laugh threatening to escape, would've crushed her. She looked like a raccoon.

Her voice was scratchy and hollow. "Fern, do you remember the day of the car wash?"

Fern dropped what she was holding. "I just had the same memory."

Britney's arms fell to her side as she scanned the room. "Remember what she said the night of the Snow Flurry Dance?"

"She said a lot of things that night." Fern stated with no emotion.

"Just said, we should make memories." Brie gripped Fern's shoulders. "Memories, Fern. She wouldn't want us huddled in the dark like this."

"I miss her so much," Fern sobbed.

Brie seemed ready to let me go. I removed my hand from

her to place both on Fern to project my thought. "I miss you too."

Fern's head snapped back and hit the wall. "What did you say?"

"She wouldn't–"

"No, you said you miss her too." Fern pushed Britney's arms away. "I heard…"

I pushed harder. "Fern, at the salon, I told you Wade was a good choice."

An audible quiver came from her. "Britney, you may think I'm crazy, but Juslynn is talking to me."

Brie rocked back. "Um, yeah. I'll get us some water."

"No, really. You weren't there at the salon when Juslynn told me she liked Wade. Thought he was good for me. She seemed happy for us." Fern used her shirt to wipe under both puffy eyes. "You told me to use a memory. I couldn't think of one and then poof, right then I recalled everything, in detail. She's here."

Feeling feverish, I gradually stood to face my Keeper. "Haste, why do I feel ill, if I'm dead?"

"You are letting go. It's an angelic act to think of others and not yourself. By helping them, you are changing as well, hence the sick feeling." He stood by the window for a few seconds, then walked reluctantly toward me. "You need to finish." He put a hand on his stomach. "Before I use the girl's toilet to deposit my selflessness."

Steadying myself, I slid down the wall and sat next to Fern. "You have to let me go. I will take our memories with me. I love you and Brie. Please tell her."

"Britney, Juslynn said she loves you and has to go." Fern stared at the darkness.

Brie scooted back and sniffed. "Ah, that's not funny."

Exhaustion gripped me as I leaned forward and placed a

hand on Britney. "Don't remember me as a fizzle stick and take Fern to the Buzz for her caffeine fix. Promise me."

Tears ran down Brie's cheeks. "I promise," she whispered through trembling lips.

Placing my hands on the floor to stand, I caught sight of the card Carter gave me. My fingers grazed the corner, knowing who I must say goodbye to next.

The emotion helped me open the card.

The girls jumped.

Well, now they knew I was here. I reread the card and snuffed the feeling to cry before Haste had a chance to make fun of me.

I leaned toward the girls and covered their eyes once more. Redirecting my thoughts, I projected, "Be there for each other. I cherish our friendship and will check on you both, from time to time, so be good." Feeling drained, I sighed. "Please let me go."

Both said, in unison, "Goodbye, Juslynn."

Haste helped me up. "I hate to say this, but as much as I would've liked the alternative to happen. You did well, Little Layer. You're on your way, angel. I'm impressed."

With my strength gone, he pulled me into an embrace. Before I could rest my head on his chest, I vanished.

CHAPTER TWENTY

Sunday, December, 25th 2016, Christmas Night.

The bells from the church off of Main Street pealed, signaling nine o'clock mass for the Christmas goers. Haste huffed. "They need to reset their clocks."

Was he comparing the time I rose with the beginning of the service?

"Really Haste, what does it matter, it's only a few minutes difference?" I thought it was amusing that a demon cared when church started. He was definitely an enigma.

My Keeper wasn't watching me, more like brooding under the tree by my grave. It was creepy since he was cloaked in shadow. I could barely make out the glow in his eyes.

Haste's silence gave me pause, but at the same time, I tried to give myself a boost of confidence. "Well, if all goes planned, tonight should be my last task, and you'll be rid of me." I tiptoed over to my graveside. "I guess we should get on with it." Closing my eyes, I willed myself to be honest with my feelings so I could let Carter go. Feeling confident, I locked on to Haste and started to make my request, "Please take me–"

He held up his hand.

I was losing my conviction. "What's the matter?"

From under the tree, two neon violet eyes narrowed. Gradually, in a pensive manner, Haste took a few steps toward me. "Is hanging out with me so bad?" There was an edginess about him, but the question had the allure of a baited hook waiting for an answer.

"To be honest, I would have to admit, not really, but we should–"

He swiped at the air as if swatting my words away. "We make a pretty good team." A sloppy half-grin formed making his eyes lose the harshness around the corners. The demon seemed as though he had lost his ability to control his emotions. Lengthy bangs covered the glow from both orbs when he dropped his head, making him appear unsure as his voice cracked, "You and me." Caught off guard by the mishap, he cleared his throat, and kept talking, "I've seen the way you've adapted to this, uh, lifestyle."

Antsy to cut my bonds to this world and move on, I snapped, "Haste, are you stalling?" Not waiting for a reply, I sighed while removing the cloak's hood so I could see him better.

Long strands of dark curls fell down my back as I shook them free from the material. Not thinking, I nervously started running my fingers through them, to calm myself down. When a hitch of breath caught my attention, I stopped raking through the curls. My eyes flew open. Haste appeared dumbstruck, and his pale complexion had a slight tinge of color under his eyes.

I became self-conscious. "Is there something on my face?" Frantically, I brushed at both cheeks.

The demon's face fell, and then he answered, "Yes, uh, no."

I stopped moving in the middle of a swipe against my cheek.

He halted with hands raised in a don't-freak-out-on-me gesture. "I've been around for a long time Juslynn, and have taken many forms. A demon's way of life can get lonely, especially if we forget the why of our existence. It was going on two hundred years of wandering when I decided to use a new tactic, and since curiosity is in my nature, I changed myself."

Skeptically, I eyed the demon before me. "Are you trying to trick me Haste? What if I use my new angel powers on you? I could–"

Eyes pleading, he rushed me. "Juslynn, I need you to hear me out. It may be hard for you to understand, especially since you know what I am." His words were harsh and swift, before turning a little wary as he continued, "I wanted to understand humans."

Growing impatient, I hinted, "If this is a ploy to keep me from saying goodbye, and ridding myself of these emotions, I'm gonna zap you." With my hands firmly placed on my hips; I opened my mouth to give him my final destination.

Then like an explosion, he was in my head.

Haste slammed me with images that flipped backward until I was watching an awkward young boy entering through the doors of my third-grade classroom. His messy onyx locks kept falling into his face. The boy looked lost and alone. After the teacher introduced him to the class, she then ushered him down the aisle and asked me to move over so we could share the desk.

He sat down next to me, and I said, "Hello, my name is Juslynn Ann Vaxton. What's yours?"

The boy eyed me then introduced himself. "My name is Hasteson Carter Watchman."

I couldn't help myself and scrunched my nose. His name came across as stuffy. "That's unfortunate. You know, I like your middle name, can I call you Carter?"

His grin was genuine. "Sure. Is it okay if I call you Ann?"

I blinked. "Why?"

"Well, you used my middle name."

"No, you can call me Juslynn." I crossed my arms and leaned on the desk.

"You want me to call you Juslynn?"

"That's my name isn't it?"

Carter was silent for a few seconds, staring at the desk, he then asked, "Do you want to be friends?"

Even at the age of seven, I understood what friendship meant. I snickered and spat into my palm. "Friends, until the end."

Shocked, bright blue eyes bore into mine.

"Are you going to shake on it?"

"You really want to be my friend?" His voice was meek.

"Well, yes. School would be lonely without a friend, right?"

He spat into his palm and reached for my hand. I remembered that I couldn't stop staring into his eyes as we shook hands to seal our friendship. Then his figure faded from the memory.

Our realities together had come full circle. The middle of my back burned with so much intensity, I thought I was going to break in half. Physically and emotionally drained, I fell to my knees sobbing in my hands. *How could I have forgotten that day?* Once I started calling him Carter, I never thought twice about it. Everyone called him… Carter.

Denial had turned my request airy, as I spoke into my hands, "Please take me to Carter."

Nothing happened. I remained on my knees near my grave.

"Juslynn, look at me."

"No!" My response was muffled.

"Please." That one simple word from him, broke my resolve.

One by one I peeled my fingers away and saw dress shoes in the snow. Lifting my head, I saw the grey tux that was burned into my memory. Carter stood in front of me, but instead of his piercing blue eyes, Haste's glowing violet orbs pleaded for understanding.

Right then, I wished my form could melt into the snow.

With a sense of urgency, Haste lowered himself to capture my attention. "For years, I tried to tell you." He paused in thought. "Eleven to be exact, I wanted to share with you my world. I don't know how I allowed you to get under my skin, but I did." He ran his fingers through his hair a few times, in a display of frustration. "When I met you, you befriended me, no questions asked. As I watched you grow up, I could feel so many emotions growing between us. But knowing what you were and what I was—meant being together would be impossible for us. Trust me, I thought of several ways I could try to change you, but I couldn't risk exposing myself or possibly placing you in danger with the other demons. Like I did at the dance."

Then I recalled the way the limo driver was acting and the strange conversation between the two of them. I couldn't look at Haste. His explanation was lost on me; I didn't fully comprehend what he was trying to explain. "Haste, what are you saying? The limo driver was a demon, like you?"

"Yes. He figured out what you were. He was also the one that sought your mother. I'm not sure if he was the one that disclosed her location to the ones that killed her."

The events in my life leading up to the night of prom began to layer over my mind. Envisioning the bathroom, I remembered Cher and the warning; I also wanted to know what was going on between the two of them.

"Is Cher a demon too?" I stood not wanting to see his reaction when I spoke about her.

His lips disappeared into a thin line. "No, Cher is what our kind calls, a Link."

"A Link? What's that?" I needed for him to explain so I wouldn't focus on the kiss they shared.

"She comes from a long line of gypsies or fortunetellers. They also can aid in connecting our kind with the living if we need to give them a message."

I frowned as I felt the heat of jealousy color my cheeks. To hide my anxiety, I started pacing the length of my grave. My hand gripped the sides of my cloak and I closed it like a protective shield.

"You want to know what Cher and I were doing that night, don't you?" There was a sense of pride in his voice. "It was work related."

"Work?"

"I made a deal with her. That's what demons do."

"She knew about you?"

He bobbed his head, inky locks swayed.

"What was the deal?"

"I wanted to know why she was bothered by you so much. She finally disclosed that she was being haunted."

"Haunted?"

"Yes, by Cerena. Your dad kept your mother bound to this plain, but on purpose. That way she could watch over you, but it became too hard on your father, so Cher accepted to have your mom attach herself to her." He laughed dryly.

"Kind of ironic that your nemesis was also one of your caretakers."

Cher's voice echoed it's warning in the back of my head.

"But why did you kiss her?"

"That was my payment for her silence and information on how you were doing."

Then it dawned on me when she told me to not freak out from certain events, and I felt stupid for not understanding what had transpired between them.

He appeared guilty. "I wanted to tell you, but it wasn't the right time. And then you caught us in the middle of our exchange. I still regret her kissing me in front of you, but it was just a deal. There were no feelings behind it, I swear."

I knew this was petty of me but I still blurted it out, "But demons lie."

"We do, but you know, deep within your heart and soul, I'm telling you the truth." He blushed a little.

"Haste—"

"Juslynn, I know you, so well. I just wish you could see me for who I am and not what I am." His approach was hesitant. "I'm not only a demon but a lost soul, Juslynn."

My prince turned out to be a demon, and I was a princess cursed to become an angel. *Could our relationship be any more complicated?*

Then he extended a hand for me to take it. I was hesitant, but he reassured me if we evened out the power charge between us, we could touch without hurting each other. Trusting him, I placed both of my hands in his as he pulled me closer. The twin tracks of electrical pain shot up both arms and into my head. Haste never let go but tightened his grip, and I thought if he could take it so could I. Our fingers intertwined with a zap and both of us winced before the charge dissipated to a steady hum.

Haste let go of my right hand and in his left, a blue rose materialized. "I have a question for you." He looked nervous.

I bit my lower lip before answering. "Yes?"

"A demons' life isn't so bad. I know I'm asking a lot of you, but please stay with me, Juslynn. I don't know how, but I fell in love with you. I have wanted to tell you for so long."

It was odd, my whole life, even my death, felt right. I was supposed to die. This was my fate. During my life, Carter was there for me. Especially, after I lost my mom, and through the aftereffects from my dad's heartache. Now, it was my turn to ease his eternal loneliness.

Was there a way for us to remain together?

My eyes ached with unshed tears as I cracked my resolve and shared my secret. "I've wanted nothing more than to be with you. I'm in love you, Hasteson."

He shivered from me using his real name. "You know, we have to seal the deal."

"What do we have to do?"

"Will you accept my," he rolled his eyes playfully, in the middle of his question, "Christmas gift?" Hasteson stepped into my personal space.

I held out my hand between us for the flower.

He flashed me, one of his, melt-on-toast smiles and my breath caught.

Like a lightning flash, the similarities between both man and demon became clear, and I felt ashamed that I never noticed my Keeper was my best friend. Guilt pushed me to apologize. "Carter, I mean, Haste…"

Eyelids lowering, he asked, "Juslynn, may I kiss you?"

A mix of shyness and revved anticipation dove into my soul.

Haste leaned in and whispered against my lips, "Juslynn Ann Vaxton, please save me."

My body responded as our lips met with a low current of warmth. Then passion swept us both under, and he deepened the kiss. Haste moaned into my mouth, and I trembled against him. My arms curled up around his neck, and he followed the same motion around my waist.

I broke the kiss long enough to whisper against his mouth, "I love you, so much."

Hasteson pulled me back to him to continue our kiss.

And with one little phrase, I lost myself to a demon that night, but in return, I gave him a gift as well, a part of me. I was unaware of this world Hasteson was a part of, but from what he explained, angel and demon pairings didn't happen unless one sacrificed themselves for the other.

In the back of my mind, I thought of all the moments I shared with Haste. Focused on the human aspect of my emotions and separated the angel side of me. Pushing my humanly desires toward Hasteson, I was hit in the middle of my shoulder blades with an intense scorching sensation, as two wings extended from my back.

As we finished our second kiss, Haste groaned, not in pleasure, but in pain. He started to buckle in my arms as my hands slid up his back to find feathers. I opened my eyes to see two huge black wings, marbled in white. They were jutting out from both shoulder blades.

Breathlessly, I asked, "Hasteson? What happened?"

I curved my wings around us for support. They were the photo negative of Hasteson's. Mine were snowy-white and marbled in black. He didn't need to explain, my silent heart told me. He had pushed into me some of his demon side and because of that, the magic we exchanged changed our fate.

I would remain a half-human, half-angel. Hasteson was now half-demon, half-human. We had found a loophole by merging. I adjusted my hold to pull him closer. *He loved me.* My happiness was on the verge of combusting.

Haste found his feet and backed away enough to meet my gaze. "Merry Christmas, Short Stuff."

I couldn't stand it and tugged him back to me suggestively. "Merry Christmas, my Keeper."

ACKNOWLEDGMENTS

First, I would like to thank my husband and kids for understanding my passion, and the need to share the stories that live within my heart. Also, to my editor, Amber Hassler, for curbing my repetitive tongue and staying up late so my stories are polished enough to shine. To my Daemonic Minions in the Unseen Street team, if it wasn't for your belief in my characters, and your passion to dive into one of their new adventures, I would be sitting in a corner, talking to myself. A huge "thanks" to you, the reader; for allowing Juslynn to share her story with you.

So, from the bottom of my storyweaving heart, "I appreciate you."

Kathy-Lynn x.x

A REAPFUL OF KATHY-LYNN CROSS

KATHY-LYNN CROSS

Once a California girl, her mother became tired of the anthill lifestyle and moved their family to Las Vegas, Nevada, where she remains firmly planted today. Her first year, college English professor opened his class with; *write what you know*, and it inspired her. Kathy-Lynn claims writing pretty much fell into her lap after that.

In 2008, her niece was hospitalized, and she wanted to do something special for her and wrote a short story about a mermaid's desire to be a guardian. The next day her niece and a few nurses wanted to know, "What was next" in the story. It was then she realized, her dream to become a Storyweaver might be possible and has been writing seriously for the past seven years.

Kathy-Lynn loves Coca-Cola red and obsessively uses it in everything; red nails make her giddy. If she hasn't wandered into the Unseen where her reapers play, she enjoys baking and cake decorating—especially around the holidays. Her favorite downtime, is spending time with her family, curled up with a cup of coffee and a good book. Kathy-Lynn lives with her husband of twenty-three years, two kids, three cats, and one thirteen-year-old, Silver-dollar fish, named Tweedle-Dee.

You can find out more on upcoming projects, new character videos, book trailers, Unseen merchandise and much more by visiting her website.

My website:

www.kathylynncross.com

More of her works and short stories are on Smashwords:

https://tinyurl.com/yc9utndj

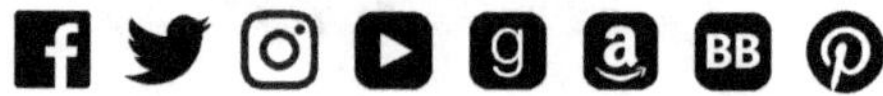

OTHER WORKS BY KATHY-LYNN CROSS

Look for the revised version of So Shall I Reap - Book One The Unseen Series.

One reaper's curiosity links her soul to him. One girl's future needs his protection. Two paths, intertwining but never connecting as they discover what being human is all about.

Book Two - To Keep Death's Vow, is available on most platforms.
The reaper is back with reinforcements.

With both Bond-Rites hanging over Tevin's cloak and the Unseen closing in on Alexcia, this reluctant reaper finds his control decomposing. Will Alexcia jeopardize what Tevin has tried to protect for the last ten years… her life?